MISSING IN ACTION

The Apache Campaign, 1885–1886

John Raffensperger, MD

Strategic Book Publishing and Rights Co.

Strategic Book Publishing and Rights Co., LLC
USA | Singapore
www.sbpra.net

For information about special discounts for bulk purchases, please contact Strategic Book Publishing and Rights Co. Special Sales, at bookorder@sbpra.net.

ISBN: 978-1-68235-521-3

Book Design: Suzanne Kelly

INTRODUCTION

The story *Reconstruction, Heal or Kill* was about Tom Slocum, a teenage boy who became a doctor's apprentice, courted an Amish girl, defended ex-slaves, and went away to medical school.

Missing in Action, the sequel, is fiction, but the characters and geographic details of the 1885–86 campaign against the Apache Indians are based on historical research as well as the author's visit to the area. I used the names of army officers and civilian scouts who were involved in the actual campaigns. The names of rivers, towns, and mountain ranges have changed over the years but are historically accurate.

Two characters in the story deserve special mention. Tom Horn, an Indian scout, cowboy, soldier, range detective and a Pinkerton agent, was a larger-than-life western character. Horn allegedly killed 14 men during his career. In 1902, he was convicted of murder and hanged in Cheyenne, Wyoming. There was doubt about his guilt and in 1993, during a mock trial, he was found innocent.

Leonard Wood, who in the story replaced Tom Slocum as a contract surgeon to the army, graduated from Harvard Medical School and started his military career as an army surgeon during the Apache campaign. When the Apaches killed the officer who commanded a troop, Wood took over and led the soldiers. He then joined the regular army and rose in rank to brigadier general. Wood commanded the Rough Riders during the Spanish-American War and afterwards became the military governor of Cuba and later the governor of the Philippines. In 1910, he became the Army Chief of Staff and was almost nominated for the presidency. Leonard Wood died with a brain tumor in 1927.

CHAPTER ONE

The Funeral

The skies darkened over the small cemetery on a hill that overlooked Sandy Ford. Black clouds rolled in from the west, and a shrieking wind sent the last yellowed leaves flying from branches. Just as people converged on the open grave, sheets of cold rain poured out of the clouds and splattered with a hollow sound on the wooden coffin.

"Damn you! Damn you all to hell!" shouted Tom Slocum.

"Thas enuff, Dr. Tom," said Isaiah.

"Blasphemer," said old man Bontrager, Rachel's father. The faces of her brothers and the Amish farmers were set in anger, not grief, over Rachel's death. They had wanted her to be buried in Amish consecrated ground. "Brother Ertle will officiate," said her father.

"No, my friend Isaiah will read the service," Tom shouted. Isaiah's worn, ebony face was serene as he looked out over the townsfolk huddled beneath umbrellas behind Dr. Slocum. Tom had delivered their babies, set broken bones, and sat with their children through feverish nights, but they edged away to their carriages. They were angry that an ex-slave would read the service rather than a minister of the gospel. Isaiah took his place at the head of the open grave with the simple coffin. Rachel's father and mother, her brothers, and the Amish farmers in their severe, simple black clothing and broad-brimmed hats became quiet out of respect for Rachel, even though she had left the Amish to marry Tom.

Isaiah removed his battered felt hat. Rain poured over his grizzled head and down his black face. His voice rolled over the cemetery:

1

*To everything there is a season, and a time to every pur-
    pose under the heaven:*
A time to be born, and a time to die;
A time to plant, and a time to pluck up that which is planted;
A time to kill, and a time to heal;
A time to break down, and a time build up;
A time to weep, and a time to laugh;
A time to mourn, and a time to dance;
*A time to cast away stones, and a time to gather stones
    together;*
A time to embrace, and a time to refrain from embracing;
A time to get, and a time to lose;
A time to keep, and a time to cast away;
A time to rend, and a time to sew;
A time to keep silence, and a time to speak;
A time to love, and a time to hate;
A time of war, and a time of peace.

Isaiah's words silenced the stony-faced Amish farmers. The blacksmith, shopkeepers, and townspeople paused and listened to the majestic words from Ecclesiastes that Isaiah recited from memory. "It is time to say farewell to our beloved Rachel and to honor Dr. Tom in his grief," Isaiah said.

The rain poured even harder out of a gloomy, late October sky. Black earth at the edge of the grave turned to mud, and rivulets poured into the grave onto the plain wood coffin. The half-drunk gravediggers backed away from the grave and staggered to their hut out of the rain.

"Leave, leave, you worthless beggars," said Tom. He furiously took up a long-handled shovel, and with rain streaming down his face and soaking his clothes, bent his back, flung his arms into the task, and grunted with the force of throwing wet clods onto his wife's coffin. He piled wet dirt into a mound over the grave well into the dusk of early evening. When it was done, the rain had turned to sleet; he wiped his face with a muddy hand, threw down the shovel, and stumbled away. His face was wet, but not with tears. Tom had vowed he would never again cry when the preacher had taken him away to the orphan-age years ago. Obediah, one of Isaiah's sons, helped Tom into the open wagon drawn by two mules and drove him to Doctor Steele's home, which doubled as a hospital.

Odette, Dr. Steele's lovely wife, met him at the door. "He would not eat," she said, tilting her head toward the young boy at her side.

The boy flung himself into Tom's arms. "I want Mother."

Tom shielded Daniel's small body as best he could, but the boy was soaked by the time they arrived at the small house where Tom and Rachel had made their home. He removed his son's wet clothing, dried him with a towel, helped him into a flannel nightgown, and carried him to the boy's attic room.

"Under the covers with you," said Tom. The boy obediently snuggled beneath the homemade quilts.

"Momma always said a prayer," said Daniel.

"Would a story do?" Tom asked. The boy turned his face to the wall with a sad noise in his throat. Tom patted his shoulder until Daniel went to sleep.

Tom sank into a chair in the living room and thought of Dr. Steele's words: "You should have known better." It had started when Rachel had returned from the one-room school where she taught farm children reading, writing, and numbers. She unhitched the mare from the buggy and led her into the stall. The mare, always nervous, sidestepped and backed Rachel against the wooden boards. Her arm scraped on a splinter. She ignored the instant jabbing pain and the drop of blood. The wound was tiny, nothing to be bothered about. After dinner, she mentioned the slight wound to Tom, who found and removed a two-inch wood splinter from under the skin on her forearm just above the wrist. They had forgotten the splinter, but two weeks later, her jaw muscles jerked and spasmed. That night, she had a fever, and by the next day, the jerking spasms had spread to her arms. She couldn't open her mouth or swallow. Tom asked his partner, Dr. Robert Steele, to see Rachel.

"It's lockjaw. You should have opened the wound to let in air when you removed the splinter," he said. Tom had turned away, damning his stupidity. By the third day, Rachel could hardly breathe, and during the final, awful night, the muscles of her back went into spasm. The force of the muscular contraction arched her back and pulled her head into a grotesque contortion. In desperation, Tom gave her an injection of morphine sulfate. The spasms relaxed, but she stopped breathing and died in his arms.

Yes, I should have opened the wound and swabbed it with carbolic, he thought. Hadn't he learned anything after years of study?

Tom had dreamed of going west to fight Indians, but then Dr. Steele came to town and convinced him that healing was better than killing. Dr. Steele had taken him on as an apprentice, and Tom learned the rudiments of medicine, how to give an ether anesthetic, and to set bones. Dr. Steele forced him to memorize *Gray's Anatomy* and to learn Latin. In 1878, when he was eighteen years old, he went off to Rush Medical College in Chicago.

He could not bear to sleep in the same bed he had shared with Rachel. It was the same bed where she had died, or had he killed her with the morphine? He had only wanted to relieve her misery.

Tom fell into the sort of reverie between sleep and wakefulness that brings back old memories. His mind drifted to his first days at the Rush Medical College in Chicago.

***

He took a room with three other students at Miss Maude's rooming house, a few blocks from the school. They were all rough farm boys but eager to learn medicine. On the first day, they bought a pot for coffee and a skillet to fry bacon and eggs for breakfast. Miss Maude gave them a stew of boiled beef with potatoes for dinner.

Rush Medical College had taken its first students in 1843, only a few years after the founding of Chicago on the banks of a river next to Lake Michigan. The school had grown, but the great fire of 1871 had destroyed the college buildings. Fortunately for Tom and his fellow students, the school had built a new, impressive five-story building next to the Cook County Hospital on Harrison Street in Chicago's west side. The tuition was seventy dollars a year, more than most students could afford. Two hundred students, both the first- and second-year classes, were in the amphitheater the first day of school. The professors repeated the same lectures every year to both classes rather than teach advanced subjects the second year.

The first lecturer, Dr. J. Adams Allen, or "Uncle Allen," as the students called him, president of the college, had white side-whiskers and wore gold spectacles perched on his nose. Dr. Allen spoke for two hours on bad humors, changes in the season, and sinful personal habits—such as the use of alcohol or tobacco—as the general causes of disease. He spent a great deal of time on diseases that resulted from illicit relations with women of ill repute. At first, Tom and the other students furiously took down the professor's every word in their notebooks. As he listened, Tom became more and more frustrated. Dr. Allen never mentioned germs, the work of Pasteur, or Lister's antiseptic surgery. He pooh-poohed the use of a stethoscope. Tom stopped taking notes. The entire lecture was contrary to everything he had learned from Dr. Steele, who had studied in Edinburgh.

Dr. Moses Gunn, professor of anatomy and surgery, introduced anatomy with a review of the body systems and finished with, "Gentlemen, tomorrow be prepared to discuss the anatomy of the upper extremity."

The next morning, the stink of a partly embalmed cadaver greeted the students. "We will commence with the osteology of the upper extremity," Professor Gunn said. "You," he pointed to a hapless student in the last row, "identify the bones of the arm and hand."

The poor fellow had a long shock of unkempt hair, farmer boots, and a black jacket over his flannel shirt. "Ah, um, well, this here is the humerus bone, and I think this is the radius." He stopped speaking; his shoulders drooped and he wiped his hand across his sweaty face.

5

"That's enough," cried Professor Gunn. "You, in the front row, come here." He pointed to Tom. Tom confidently started with the scapula, the clavicle, and went down the arm, touching each bone as he recited their names. When he finished with the small metacarpal bones at the wrist, the students burst out in applause.

"Perhaps you can tell us the signs and symptoms of a fracture of the navicular bone," said Professor Gunn.

Tom thought for a moment and extended his hand, with the thumb stretched back. "There is pain and swelling in the wrist and tenderness here in the snuffbox." He pointed to the depression just at the base of the thumb.

"Remarkable, truly remarkable," said Professor Gunn.

At the end of the class, students crowded around Tom. "How could you remember all those little bones?" they asked.

"Easy, I use a mnemonic," said Tom.

"What's that?" they asked, almost in unison.

"Never Lower Tillie's Pants, Grandmother Might Come Home; the first letters remind me of Navicular, Lunate, Triquetrum, Pisiform, Greater Multangular, Multangular, Capitate, Hamate. There, it's easy," Tom said.

A boy with a shock of blond hair put out his hand. "I flunked anatomy twice. They will kick me out if I flunk again. Could you tutor some of us in anatomy?" he asked.

Tom hardly hesitated. "I can tutor six students for two bits apiece for each session, but you must find a cadaver," Tom said.

"That's easy," said a tall, black-haired fellow.

"Will you dig up a grave?" Tom asked.

"Naw, the pauper's cemetery is too far away. Besides, all that digging is a lot of work. For a bottle of whisky, the guy who hauls bodies from the county morgue will let us have any cadaver we want. Come with us to the alley back of the morgue about six tomorrow morning," the black-haired fellow said.

The next morning, the boys gave the driver—an ancient Swede—the bottle, opened a pine box, put the body of a middle-aged man in a handcart, covered it with an old quilt, and hauled it to the coal shed behind Miss Maude's boarding house. The boys doused the already-stinking corpse with formaldehyde. Miss Maude complained about the smell, but the boys brought in buckets of coal and armloads of kindling wood for the stoves.

For the next month, Tom dissected and drilled his fellow students until every boy could identify the muscles, nerves, arteries, and veins in the body. When the students had reduced the body to a few shreds of bone and muscle, they buried it in a trash heap. Tom earned enough money to pay for his board and room and for study in Edinburgh and Vienna.

***

The fire was out and the oil lamp was spluttering when a wild knock on the door awoke Tom from his reverie.

CHAPTER TWO

A Country Practice

"**D**oc, the missus been havin' pains since yesterday, and the baby ain't a comin'. Ya gotta help us right now." Dick Stevens shivered, despite a fur cap pulled down over his ears and a heavy sheepskin coat that hung to his knees. The rain had stopped, but it had turned cold, bitter cold. Stevens was a stooped, rawboned farmer who had, for ten years, tried to make a living on forty acres of prairie ten miles north of Sandy Ford.

"Anyone with the missus?" Tom asked.

"Widow Blake," Stevens said.

The widow was an old midwife who absolutely refused to wash her hands before delivering babies. Tom had given her a solution of dilute carbolic to rinse her hands, but she had never uncorked the bottle.

"Hitch up the buggy while I get ready," Tom said.

"It done froze a crust. Never get through in a buggy. You gotta ride horseback," said Stevens.

"I hate to ride, but go on and saddle Old Jack, the black gelding, out in the stable while I get ready," Tom said.

He took a sheet and towels that Rachel had heated in the oven to kill germs. It was a trick he had learned from the surgeons in Vienna, which was more effective than soaking in carbolic. Next, he took the worn black leather bag with the instruments, bottles of carbolic, and ether from the shelf and finally dressed in thick woolen pants and a long sheepskin coat. Outside, the stars were bright as diamonds, and a quarter moon hung in the western sky. He packed the saddlebags, scratched the big horse's ears, and climbed on the saddle. From long habit, Old Jack followed the other horse on the dirt road leading north.

Tom swayed with the horse's gait and fell into a half sleep. His mind again drifted back to the pleasant days at Rush:

***

He had memorized enough chemistry to get by and had listened intently to De Laskie Miller's lectures on obstetrics. During the second year, he skipped most classes and tagged along with the interns at the Cook County Hospital to learn the latest surgical techniques. The hospital was brand new, but the wards stunk with pus and surgical gangrene. The surgeons didn't believe in germs, and every wound became infected. Things improved with the arrival of Christian Fenger, a sad-eyed Dane who had been a surgeon in the Franco-Prussian War and had studied pathology and bacteriology in Vienna. The interns and students eagerly followed him to learn the latest European techniques. Tom and the others crowded into the morgue and watched Fenger minutely examine each organ and cut thin slices of tissue to study under a microscope. It was a revelation to see a lung full of pus from a patient with pneumonia or a cancer of the bowel that had caused bleeding from the gut.

A few young surgeons took up Lister's carbolic spray and swabbed wounds with carbolic, but they still wore blood-crusted frock coats while doing surgery, and if they dropped an instrument, they picked it up and kept on operating. When the wounds became infected, they claimed the Lister treatment didn't work. Fenger was a slow, meticulous, scrupulously clean surgeon. His patients recovered without infections. "Ach, eef you want to learn scientific medicine, go to Germany," he said.

***

A howling dog awoke Tom from his restless dream. The low log cabin sat beneath a bluff in a grove of trees. While Stevens stabled the horses, Tom entered the low-ceilinged cabin. The air was smoky from a smoldering fireplace. Muddy footprints were

9

encrusted on the plank floor; dirt gathered in every corner, and a stack of greasy dishes lay on the kitchen counter.

The Widow Blake wrung her hands. "She done already lost three babies, and she been bleedin' for most on to a week. I tried hard 'cause they was a-lookin' forward to a young-un," she said.

The poor patient was small like her husband and not young. Her lined face and roughened hands showed years of hard work. Tom had no more than removed his coat when she stretched her arms, grabbed the bedposts, and uttered a long, drawn-out scream. "Oh God, take it! Take it. Oh God, please!" Tom quickly rinsed his hands in carbolic and examined her. The cervix, the outlet of the uterus, was almost completely closed, and just inside the uterus he felt the soft, spongy tissue of the placenta.

"The placenta, the afterbirth, is blocking the birth canal," said Tom.

"You jes got to do something," Widow Blake said.

"I will have to cut and take it," Tom said. He had seen Caesarean sections in Edinburgh and Vienna and had once helped Dr. Steele, but that was in the hospital, with good lights. It was, as one surgeon said, "Cut until you see the baby, take out the baby, and sew up everything you cut."

Mrs. Stevens screamed again, just as her husband clumped into the room. "I can't stand it no more," he said. "I'll wait in the barn."

Tom pulled a table to the middle of the room. "Put every candle and the oil lamp on that shelf in front of the mirror," Tom said. He put the instruments in a carbolic solution, and when they had placed Mrs. Stevens onto the table, he washed her abdomen and rinsed his hands. He then put on an apron over his clothing and covered the patient with a sheet.

"Pour the ether, one drop at a time, on the gauze until she goes to sleep," Tom said. Mrs. Stevens coughed and choked at first, then took rapid, sobbing breaths and fell asleep.

"That's fine, slow the drops," Tom said.

He took a deep breath, then selected a razor-sharp, wooden-handled scalpel from the soaking instruments and made a long incision from belly button to pubis. Her abdominal wall was thin, and within a minute, his knife was down to the bulging, dark red uterus. His first cut into the uterus was slow and tentative, then he went deeper until fluid gushed out of the wound. He enlarged the opening until he felt a small arm; the incision wasn't large enough for the head. Tom cut again, mostly by feel, until he found the head. The clear amniotic fluid became bloody. *Oh God, is the placenta coming loose?* He pulled the baby from the uterus, clamped the umbilical cord, and laid the babe across the mother's legs. It was a boy, but he didn't breathe and turned blue. There was another gush of blood. Tom gently removed the placenta and squeezed the uterus as hard as possible. With his other hand, he slapped the baby's buttocks. There was a feeble cry, but the baby was still blue.

"Missus Blake, stop the ether and care for the babe," Tom said. She came around the table, picked up the dying child, gave him a slap on the back, and squeezed his chest. There was a feeble cry, then another, stronger. Tom massaged the uterus until the bleeding slowed to a trickle.

"Oh, oh," the new mother moaned.

"Lie still. Take deep breaths. It's almost over," Tom said. He passed a large, curved needle with linen thread from one side of the uterine incision to the other, tied the knot, and wove the suture, zigzag fashion, until the incision was closed.

She threw her hands in the air. "Mrs. Stevens, lie very still. The baby is fine," Tom said. He swabbed the open wound with gauze soaked in carbolic and then sutured the muscles and skin. By the time he had finished, the candles had nearly guttered out, and the charred wick of the oil lamp smoked. Tom put the dressing soaked in a carbolic solution over the wound and sighed, "It's all over."

Missus Blake put the baby to the mother's breast, where he sucked the rich, creamy first milk. Tom went to the door and shouted, "Stevens, you got a boy!"

When they moved her from table to bed, a growing pool of blood spread between her legs. The mother was limp, pale, and at the point of death. Her pulse was too rapid to count. Tom

11

again massaged the uterus, but it was flaccid and would not clamp down to stop the bleeding.

"I got just the thing," Missus Blake said. She poured a half cup of dark brown liquid from an old whisky bottle and forced a spoonful into the new mother's mouth.

"What is it?" Tom asked.

"Hawthorne leaf and cinnamon," Widow Blake said.

Most doctors would have scorned the old folk remedy, but Tom's father had collected roots and leaves to make medicines that often worked better than remedies used by doctors. Within minutes after drinking the remedy, the bleeding slowed and stopped.

Dick Stevens paced the floor, getting in the way and shouting, "You save her, or, by damn, I'll lick the tar out of you!" he said.

"Damn your hide, get to work. Boil water for strong coffee with lots of sugar and make soup," Tom said.

Tom sunk into a wooden chair and held his head in his hands. *She will almost surely die from blood loss—another failure*, he thought.

After a half hour of dark musing, he stood, stretched, and gathered the instruments and bloody towels into a bundle. "Make her drink the coffee."

With Dick Stevens holding her almost upright, the Widow Blake forced the hot coffee with molasses down the patient's throat. She gulped, choked, but took the entire cup. "Wait a few minutes and then give her soup," Tom ordered.

"Ain't got no soup, but there's some beef stew left," said Stevens.

"Add some water and give her the liquid," Tom said. He felt the uterus again. It was firm and clamped down. The bleeding had stopped, and she had a stronger pulse.

A rooster crowed in the barnyard when Tom was finally satisfied with both mother and baby. He packed the instruments and linen in saddlebags and mounted Old Jack. Stevens came out of the barn with two red chickens tied together at the feet. "I ain't got no money, but you kin have these two good eatin' hens," he said.

"Tie 'em behind the saddle," Tom said. "I'll be back tomorrow or the next day for sure. You better have the cabin spick-and-span clean and those dishes washed with laundry soap or I'll whale the tar out of you," Tom said.

Stevens hung his head. "I'll do better."

Tom put Old Jack to a trot down the low hill beneath skeletal branches of white oaks that were starkly outlined against the lightening sky. The stars were fading, and there was a faint glow on the line of trees that marked the river to the east. When he came down to the road through the bottomland that led to Sandy Ford, Tom halted the horse and gazed at the dead stalks of corn tilted crazily in a field. The color reminded him of Rachel's hair. The black cloud of her death still hung over him, but the operation had buoyed his spirits. *A life taken and a life given*, he thought. A family of black-masked raccoons skittered into the brush, and a great horned owl glided noiselessly across the road. A long V-shaped skein of ducks, quacking noisily, flew from the fields toward the river, where they would rest with heads under their wings during the day. *The night critters are going home to bed*, Tom thought.

Old Jack's hooves broke through the icy crust of mud, but he clopped along at a good pace. He was eager for his warm stall and a nose bag of oats. It was cold, but the crisp air felt good. Tom was wide awake and enjoying the sights of the fresh morning. A rabbit scampered down a row of corn stalks, and a covey of quail sat in a circle, their beaks all pointing inward. He was nearly halfway home when the sun separated from the horizon and cast long shadows over the land. A quarter mile ahead, the road dipped into a shallow ravine lined with willows and cottonwood trees along Coffee Creek. A few yards further on, he saw a horse in the shadows under a cottonwood tree. The horse's head drooped, and he kept shifting his weight from the left front hoof. There was no sign of a rider. A flock of ducks circled the creek and set their wings as if to light on the water. The birds flared up on frantically beating wings and flew toward the river. *Something scared those ducks*, Tom thought. He pulled on the reins until Old Jack halted. Tom squinted hard at the line of trees and thought a shadow moved behind the cottonwood where the horse was tied. He turned in the saddle, unfastened the saddlebag, and found the old cap-and-ball Colt revolver that his friend Mr. Birt had carried at Shiloh. Tom half-cocked the pistol and slipped it into his coat pocket. Old Jack whinnied in greeting to the gray mare just as the muzzle of a sawed-off Harpers Ferry musket poked out from behind the tree.

"Throw up your hands, mister. I want that horse and your money." The high-pitched, squealy voice came from a rail-thin young fellow with light, rust-colored hair that reached his shoulders from beneath a slouch hat. He was hardly more than a boy and wore a lightweight cloth jacket over a flannel shirt and denim pants stuck into knee-high cowhide boots.

Tom rested his hands, still holding the reins, on the pommel and looked at the boy with an unflinching stare. "Be careful, or that thing will explode and take your head off," he said.

The boy was shivery, and the muzzle of the old rifle wobbled. The boy's teeth chattered, as much from nervousness as cold. "I ain't sayin' it again; put up your hands and get down off that horse or I'll blow a hole right through your gut," the boy said.

Tom took his right foot out of the stirrup and threw his leg over the horse. The two chickens set up a squawk and flapped their wings. The boy turned the rifle toward the chickens. "What the hell," he said.

Tom put both feet on the ground, drew his pistol, and leaned under Old Jack's neck. The boy touched the trigger; the old musket made a *phoo* sort of noise and belched a cloud of smoke. A load of birdshot rolled out of the barrel.

"Your powder was wet. What the hell do you think you are doing?" Tom asked. The boy sat down, leaned against the cottonwood tree, and covered his face with both hands.

"I didn't mean to shoot nobody. The gun just went off."

"Those muskets had a hard trigger pull," Tom said.

"Pa filed down the tang," the boy said.

Tom picked up the musket, cocked the hammer, and touched the trigger. "Damn thing does have a hair trigger. What's your name and where are you headed?" Tom asked.

14

"Ezekiel Becker. I'm a goin' west but ain't got no money and the horse went lame," he said.

"How old are you?"

"Pertnear sixteen," the boy said.

"Why aren't you at home?" Tom asked.

"Ain't got no home. Paw and maw died with the flux." The ragged boy heaved with sobs.

"They must call you Zeke. How long has your horse been lame?"

"She started limpin' yestidy afternoon."

Tom let down the hammer of the pistol and put it in his coat pocket. He knelt and lifted the hoof of the gray horse. "You damn fool, been ridin' this horse when she has a stone in her hoof. Bring the black case from the saddlebag," Tom said.

He pried out the stone with forceps and a curette while the boy held the hoof. "See the pus under the stone. This poor animal has been in pain," he said. The horse flinched when Tom cleaned the abscess, applied carbolic ointment, and wrapped the hoof with a cloth bandage. "The old girl will make it to town. Get up behind me and lead her."

It was almost midmorning when they arrived at Tom's house. "Put the horses in the stable; feed and rub them down. The two hens can go in the pen with the other chickens, then come in the kitchen," Tom said.

The fires had gone out, and the house was cold. Young Daniel, still in his nightshirt, was shivering in the kitchen. "Where's Mum?" he sobbed.

Oh God, I forgot my own son, Tom thought. Always, always, Rachel had been there to take care of Daniel when he went out on calls. She was gone. Tom held the boy in his arms and rocked back and forth. "I'm sorry, Dan, Mother is gone. She isn't coming back. Let's get you dressed in warm clothes, and then we'll have breakfast."

Zeke Becker came to the kitchen door. "I took care o' the horses," he said.

"Bring in a load of firewood and get the kitchen stove going," Tom said. By the time he had dressed young Dan in

15

warm clothes, the chill was gone and the stove was hot. Tom got oatmeal and milk for Dan and fixed coffee, bacon, and eggs.

"Zeke, if you are hungry, come and get it," Tom said. "I figure you are a good fellow who's had some bad luck. If you shovel out the barn and give the horses fresh hay, you can sleep in the barn tonight. There is a buffalo robe in the buggy."

"I'm grateful," Zeke replied.

"Mama always said grace," said Daniel. Tom muttered a short prayer, and then they all pitched into the food. Tom was bone-tired and felt like a beat dog because he hadn't looked after his son. What would he do? Life with Rachel had been so good. With her Amish cooking, he had put on weight and wasn't the same bone-thin kid he had been years ago. She had kept the house spick-and-span, but already there were boot marks on the floor and dust on the tables.

A horse pulling a buggy clopped to the front door. "Whoa, whoa, there," a voice said.

Tom answered the knock. It was Walter, Rachel's youngest brother, and his wife, Miriam. Both wore Amish black. "Can we talk?" Walter asked.

"Come in," Tom said. Walter and Miriam were the only family members who had so much as talked with Rachel after their marriage. Tom always thought they could have been friends had it not been for the anger and opposition of the rest of the Bontragers.

"How do you aim to take care of the boy?" Walter asked.

"Haven't had time to think it out. Figure I'll find a house-keeper," Tom replied.

"We want to take him," Miriam said.

"Take him from me?" Tom asked.

Miriam turned red in the face. "You could see him," she said.

"Your family would never let me near your place."

"We would bring him to town," Walter said.

Daniel left the table and climbed onto Miriam's lap. "I want my mother," he said. His arms went around the pleasant-faced woman. Miriam wiped oatmeal off his face with a handkerchief and kissed him. Tom slumped and hung his head. The Bontrager family had big, rambling, comfortable houses surrounded by great trees and near a good fishing creek. Their barns were filled with horses and cows; there were pens with chickens and banty roosters. Rachel had her own horse before her accident and had raced across the fields; Daniel could have his own pony and learn to love horses, just like his mother. Miriam and Walter had four children; one was near Daniel's age. The thought hung heavy in his mind. He massaged his temples, trying to drive away the dull pain in his head. Miriam and Walter could care for Daniel far better than he could, even with a housekeeper.

"I want to see him every week, and he must have an education. When he is twelve years old, let him decide if he wants to come and live with me," Tom said.

Walter Bontrager moved uneasily and looked at Miriam. "We will bring him up in the Amish faith," he said.

Tom collected Daniel's clothing and toys. There was a wooden horse that Isaiah had carved out of black walnut and a lead Union soldier dressed in blue and carrying a musket. Walter put the small bundle of Daniel's belongings in the back of the buggy. Tom hugged the boy, wrapped him in a thick wool blanket, and put him on the seat between Miriam and Walter. "Aunt Miriam will be your mother, but I will always be your father," he said.

17

CHAPTER THREE

Billy Malone is Missing in Action

It was Dr. Steele's turn to make country rounds, so Tom saw the townspeople. Dr. Steele's home, at the edge of town, was also their medical office and hospital. At one time, the rambling three-story house had been a station on the Underground Railroad, where fugitive slaves found refuge before going on north to freedom. That is how Odette, Dr. Steele's wife, an octoroon, the daughter and slave of a Louisiana colonel, had found her way upriver to Dr. Steele.

Obediah took his horse and buggy to the stable around back, and Odette met Tom at the door. "Oh, Tom, Dr. Steele could have taken care of the patients when he returned. You didn't have to work today," she said.

"It's fine. I would rather work than sit home and fret," Tom said.

The patients came, one by one, into the office, bobbed their heads, and mumbled, "Sorry about your wife," and then went on to describe their aches and pains. He gave Mrs. Jones a new bottle of digitalis root for her swollen ankles and heart failure, an extract of willow bark to Herman Forrest for his painful joints, and jars of carbolized salve to folks with itchy skin.

The tousle-headed five-year-old boy had red eyes and was covered with small, itchy pustules. "Doctor, is it smallpox?" his mother asked.

"Just the chicken pox. He will be good as new in a few days. Make up a gallon of water with a tablespoon each of salt and soda, soak a towel in the mixture, and put it on his skin for the itch," Tom said.

Bill Longman, a soldier at Shiloh and Vicksburg, wobbled into the small office on unsteady feet. He was bleary-eyed and his nose dripped. Bill put a hand on his upper belly and groaned. "Doc, the pain is getting worse. And I had the fits last night."

Tom felt his knobby, enlarged liver. "Ow, that hurts," Bill said.

"You damn fool, you still drink homemade rotgut whisky," Tom said.

"Just a little to calm my nerves," Bill replied.

"A little? Closer to a quart a day," Tom said.

Bill fidgeted and hung his head. "I still hear those cannon at night. Dead boys all shot to pieces march through my room. When I try to quit, I see snakes too," Bill said.

Tom watched a pair of sparrows fighting over crumbs beneath the elm tree in the yard. It was like this with a lot of veterans. They never got over the horrors, but people looked back on Lincoln's War as a great and noble cause. At one time, Tom had wanted to go off and fight Indians, but he chose medicine instead. Something stirred in his mind. The call to go west and find adventure was still there. His best friend, Billy Malone, had gone to West Point and was now an officer in faraway Arizona. He snapped out of his reverie. "I know it is hard, Bill, but cut down a little every day. When you get down to a half-pint, you can quit and not see the snakes. Those cannon will always be with you, but the drink makes it worse." Tom took a pint bottle filled with a clear liquid from the shelf. "Here is a new German medicine. Take a tablespoon every night to help you sleep."

Bill uncorked the bottle and sniffed the contents. "Lord almighty, this stuff stinks," he said.

"Take it anyway; it is paraldehyde. It will stop the fits and help you sleep, but you must cut down on the whisky," Tom said.

When Tom had finished seeing patients, Dr. Steele was back from rounds and it was time for dinner. Odette cooked with a New Orleans flair. It was really chicken cooked in wine, but Odette said it was "coq au vin." When they had finished the apple pie, Dr. Steele clipped the end of a cigar, rolled it between his fingers, struck a match, and puffed until the cigar glowed. He peered at Tom through a cloud of fragrant, blue smoke, poured two brandies, and gazed into the flames dancing in the great fireplace. "Tom, take it easy for a few days. You might even go to Chicago and visit the hospitals," Dr. Steele said.

"I might go west and look up Billy Malone," Tom responded.

"You always wanted to fight Indians," Dr. Steele said.

Tom sniffed the brandy and took a small sip. "I must go away for at least a while."

"Don't do anything hasty. Things are looking up; the farmers are getting decent prices for their corn and hogs. Just yesterday, I took a wen off a farmer's head, and he shelled out two silver dollars. I had counted on you being here so I could go to Europe to see what the German doctors are up to. There is a fellow in Switzerland who is taking out the whole thyroid for goiters," Dr. Steele said.

"Folks won't trust me after I couldn't even save my own wife. I can't stay and face these people," Tom said.

"It wasn't your fault; everyone knows there is no cure for lockjaw."

Tom finished the brandy at one gulp. "I always hankered to go west. Billy Malone is out there with the army, galloping around, chasing Indians. The Apaches are still causing trouble. I figure on talking to Mr. Birt. He always knows what's going on," Tom said.

When Tom drove the buggy into the barn, there was a rustling in the hay. Zeke Becker threw off the buffalo robe and rubbed the sleep out of his eyes. "I'll unhitch the mare 'n rub her down," he said.

"I figured you would have skedaddled out of here," Tom said.

"I ain't got no place to go. Looks like you could use some help. I'll work for food and a sleepin' place if you'll have me," the boy said.

"Come in the kitchen when you are done with the horse," Tom said.

The boy wolfed down a hunk of pork roast between two slices of homemade bread and finished off the pot of beans that had been left on the stove before Rachel's funeral. "If you are willing to take care of horses and do chores, you can stay a while," Tom said.

"I'll do most anythin'. You been good to me," the boy said.

In the morning, Zeke drove the buggy down Main Street at a good clip. Ladies were buying ribbons and frills at Otto's Variety Store; men were lined up at the new bank to deposit money; the blacksmith was busy making horseshoes and fixing plows.

"Pull up at the newspaper office," Tom said. The Klan had burned Paul Birt's building back in '78, but he had rebuilt a fine red-brick edifice with a brand new Campbell steam printing press. He put the *Sandy Ford News Democrat* out every week, just like clockwork. Mabel Shultz sat in the front office and glowered at a half dozen of Sandy Ford's most stalwart citizens. Mabel collected the gossip and wedding and funeral announcements from the whole county and sold advertisements to the local businessmen.

The frock-coated locals cajoled Mabel for news and fished for juicy morsels of gossip while waiting for the weekly paper to emerge from the press room. Walt Duke hit the spittoon just off-center with a stream of brown tobacco juice, but a gob splashed on Mabel's clean linoleum floor.

Mabel shook her fist. "That's going to cost you a full-page ad in the next edition!" she howled at the top of her lungs.

"Now, Mabel, a little tobacco juice never hurt a thing, might even do you some good," Mr. Duke said.

When Tom entered, the room went quiet. "Sorry about your wife, Tom, a great tragedy," Hiram Hunter, the lumberman, said. There were more mutterings of sympathy until Paul Birt brought out a bundle of fresh newspapers under the stump of his amputated arm.

"Guess you heard the news about Billy," he said.

"Billy? Billy Malone? What happened to my good friend?" Tom asked.

"A wire from the war department said Lieutenant William Malone is missing in action while engaging hostiles in the Arizona Territory," Mr. Birt said.

"He was chasing those damn murderin' savages," Ed Sterrett muttered.

Tom buried his head in his hands and could barely repress a great sob. This was too much. Billy had been his best friend and companion in many scrapes. "It said he was missing in action, not dead?" Tom asked.

"The wire didn't give any details," Mr. Birt said.

"In the war, missing in action was about the same as saying the fella was dead," Ed Sterrett replied.

"It's those no-good Apache Indians. The army ought to hang every damn one of them," Mr. Duke said.

"Hell, the army can't even catch them," Hiram Hunter said.

"He can't be dead. Billy was too smart and too good to die," Tom said.

The men turned away and unfolded their October 26, 1885, newspaper. The front-page headline took their attention: Vice President Thomas A. Hendricks, Age Sixty-Six, Near Death at His Home in Indianapolis.

"Ain't that a shame. For a Democrat, Hendricks was honest, even if he sympathized with the South" Mr. Duke said. The conversation turned to politics and the end of Reconstruction in the South. Tom bolted out the door and into the buggy.

"I have to get out in the country and think. Drive on across the bridge," Tom said. Zeke snapped the reins and started the mare down the street, where they waited for a steamboat to pass under the new swing bridge. When the span closed, they trotted across the wood planks to the low, muddy road that led through the sloughs and backwaters of the river to the hills a mile or so away.

It turned out to be one of those warm, sunny fall days that makes a person think summer isn't over yet. Sun sparkled on a backwater slough, and a hopeful, lost frog sat on the leaf of a water lily and belched a lonely croak.

22

"Whoa, up by that hickory tree. One day, Billy Malone got three squirrels out of that tree, shot every one in the head," Tom said.

"He musta been a crack shot," Zeke replied.

"I don't think Billy is dead. He knew how to take care of himself, unless he lost it all at West Point," Tom said.

The dirt road ran between the river and a range of low hills. "Fine bottomland, rich soil," Zeke said.

"Turn into that lane by the split rail fence," Tom said.

They came to a cabin with a well-swept dirt yard where a half dozen Negro children played with a hoop. Beyond the house was a field of harvested corn where pigs rooted for leftover kernels in the muddy ground. "This is Old Isaiah's house. He and his family were once slaves, but Captain Trimmer brought them from Virginia and set them free before the war. Miz Trimmer, his wife, gave them the property when she died," Tom said.

"Damn, it ain't right these people have a better farm than my paw," Zeke said.

"They are good people. Old Isaiah pulled me out of a snowbank and saved my life a few years back. Ask the children to get a bucket of oats for the horse while I go in and see Isaiah's wife."

The old lady was on a pallet by the fire, covered with a quilt. "Doctah Tom, you didn' hafta come all the way out here so soon after Rachel died," she said.

"Now, Isabell, I figured your boil was just about ready," Tom said.

The back of her neck was red and swollen like a big ripe tomato. "It has softened in the middle. Time to drain the pus," Tom said.

"Is you gwine to cut me? You know I don't like cuttin' and all that pain."

Tom set out a curved bistoury, probes, and forceps on a clean towel and swabbed the back of her neck with carbolic. "You just lie on your belly, hold this cloth over your face, breathe the chloroform, and you won't feel a thing," Tom said.

She took a half dozen deep breaths and giggled. "I feel dizzy already," she said.

"Good. Keep breathing." Tom waited another half minute, then made an X-shaped incision over the swelling, swabbed away thick yellow pus, probed the depths of the abscess, and broke up locules of thick pus. He finished by leaving a gauze drain, soaked in carbolic, in the depths of the wound. The operation lasted hardly more than five minutes. Isabell's hand, with the gauze soaked in chloroform, had fallen away from her face.

"When you goin' to start the cutting?" she asked.

"It's all done," Tom said.

"Doctah Tom, have some fresh corn bread with butter and gooseberry jam and coffee before you go," said Maybelle, Obediah's wife.

"I would like that just fine," Tom said.

Zeke slapped the horse with the reins. The buggy moved out of the yard and into the lane that ran between the neat fields. "I don't keer what you say. It ain't right that those people have land."

"Ezekiel, don't you ever talk like that again. Isaiah's family worked hard, cleared this land, planted, and harvested with their own hands. They deserve every bit of it. Now, get on home. We got to change horses so I can see Mrs. Stevens this afternoon," Tom said.

The new mother was weak but she smiled. The baby suckled at her breast with great vigor. Her wound was clean, and there was no sign of the postpartum sepsis that carried away many women after childbirth. Dick Stevens had cleaned the place, and Mrs. Blake had made a rich stew with corn and chicken. Tom heaved a sigh, relieved that all was well. "Well, Mrs. Blake, there is no infection. You better start using the carbolic solution on all your deliveries," he said.

Rachel's cries of agony haunted the bedroom. Tom again tossed and rolled on the couch until exhaustion overcame his overheated brain. He fell asleep, but in the deep of the night, he awoke, drenched in sweat and with a pounding heart. He lurched off the couch and fumbled for a Lucifer to light a can-

24

dle. The wavering flame cast shadows that danced like ghosts on the wall. In his nightmare, he had seen a body lowered into a fresh grave, though the people around the grave were not in Amish black but were strangers wearing uniforms. He opened the coffin to find not Rachel, but the distorted, tortured face of Billy Malone, his best friend. Tom had hardly had a drink of hard liquor since he married Rachel, but he went to the shelf, pushed aside his worn copy of *Gray's Anatomy*, and found the hidden pint bottle of whisky. He took a long swallow, but the raw alcohol burned his throat. He threw the bottle into the hearth. It crashed and splintered. *That is not the way; I will go find him,* he thought.

CHAPTER FOUR

To St. Looie with Captain Bart

Dr. Steele took a generous sip of New Orleans coffee, then wiped egg off his chin. "Have another beignet. Odette made them just for you," he said. Tom popped another of the sugary New Orleans pastries into his mouth and drained his coffee.

"Billy ain't dead. I aim to find him," Tom said.

"If he is dead, it won't make any difference if you run off into that godforsaken desert. If he is alive, the army will find him. I can't handle the practice by myself, and Tom, you are getting to be a fine surgeon. One of these days, you will be the top man in the state," Dr. Steele said.

Odette bustled into the dining room with her usual mix of French and New Orleans elegance, poured fresh, fragrant coffee, then kissed Dr. Slocum on his forehead. "Oh Tom, we can't get along without you. There is so much work," she said.

"Billy is somewhere in that desert. I dreamed that he looked up from a coffin and called to me," Tom replied.

Dr. Steele clipped the end of a cigar and lit a Lucifer but held the match until it burned out, staring at the ceiling. "Things come back to haunt us. When I flung down my rifle at Cold Harbor, the captain was going to hang me for desertion, but instead, I joined the stretcher-bearers to bring in the wounded. Grant wouldn't admit that Bobby Lee had him beat and didn't declare a truce for three days. Three days, mind you, those boys laid out there with the vultures peckin' out their eyes before we could get them. They had been proud soldiers, now they were all rotten dead. I won't ever forgive Grant, or Lincoln either. The damn war was all wrong. The labor battalion dug a big hole, and we put those poor boys to rest, Rebs and Union all together. I thought for sure I saw the lips of one of those boys movin', so I climbed over bodies to bring him back, but he was stiff dead. I still dream about those lips moving. Mebbe I didn't get to him fast enough. Tom, don't you believe in dreams, not one bit. And another thing, those Reb boys weren't no worse and no better than us Union soldiers. I 'spect the Indians are the same. They can't be all bad. We treated the Indians worse than the Rebs. At least we didn't kill Southern women and children. We stole Indian land, killed the buffalo, penned them on reservations in the most godforsaken, useless land in the country, and gave them whisky. Before you pass judgment on the Apaches, look at it from their angle," Dr. Steele said.

"I aim to go, no matter what," Tom said.

"If you have it all settled, how are you going to get there? The Arizona Territory is far away," Odette said.

"I haven't given it any thought, but railroads must go in that direction," said Tom.

Dr. Steele leaned back in his chair. "Matter of fact, there is a new railroad, the Southern Pacific, starts in New Orleans, goes through Texas all the way to California. It passes right close to the Mexican boundary."

"I could take a steamboat to New Orleans. Always wanted to see more of the river," Tom said.

"If you are set on going, we better settle up," Dr. Steele said.

"I have enough for a start, and I can make a living doctoring in the territories," Tom said.

"No, you have fifty dollars coming to you, and I will give you another fifty for your horses," Dr. Steele said.

"Thank you," replied Tom.

"You might need to pay the Indians to release Billy. You can make money playing poker if you are careful. That's how I got through school and had enough for Edinburgh."

"Yes, sir, I learned a lot from watching you and played some in school, but I didn't gamble after I married Rachel," Tom said.

"Do you know the rules and how to play a hand?" Dr. Steele asked.

"Yes, sir, I studied it some."

"Winning is a lot like studying patients. Watch for the guy who is bluffing. See who has a twitchy eye and a little tremor. If you watch the neck, you can sometimes count the pulse by the carotid artery. A rapid pulse is a sure sign of nervousness. At the same time, control your own feelings. Don't let on if you have a good hand."

"Sounds too risky. I don't like risks," Tom said.

Dr. Steele tossed a deck of cards on the table. "Won't hurt to practice. Never know when it might come in handy," Doc Steele said.

The schedule for steamboats tacked on the bulletin board in the newspaper office listed the arrivals and departures of boats for St. Louis, Peoria, Ottawa, and points north. None were scheduled to go all the way downriver to New Orleans, but the *Beaver*, captained by Bart Daniels, would leave for St. Louis at noon the next day.

"We ain't got much time to pack," Tom said.

"What about me? I always wanted to go west and fight Injuns," Zeke Becker said.

"You won't be fighting Indians but will carry bags and look after horses," Tom said.

Zeke had a pleading look in his eyes. "I'll do most anythin' if you'll take me," he said.

"Fine. Put the horses and the buggy in the barn behind Dr. Steele's house, and have the livery pick us up with a buggy at eleven tomorrow morning," Tom said. Tom packed his fine German scalpels, forceps, artery clamps, probes, curettes, two long amputation knives, and a bone saw along with an assortment of sewing needles and spools of ligatures in his large instrument case. He put towels, bottles of ether, chloroform, and carbolic solutions between layers of clothing in a large carpet bag. He looked for a long time at a picture of Rachel and Daniel, then took it from the frame and laid it on top of his clothing. Almost as an afterthought, he tucked the old cap-and-ball .31 caliber Colt with a pouch of powder and a bag of lead balls in the bag.

The steamboat landing at the foot of Edward Street was crowded with drays and wagons loaded with lumber bound for St. Louis. Roustabouts tried to herd a couple dozen fat hogs into a pen on the main deck, but the hogs snorted and pushed back like they missed the wallow back home. Bart Daniels, owner and captain of the *Beaver*, stood outside the pilothouse shouting instructions. The red scar that went halfway around his neck throbbed each time he hurled another curse at the workmen. A few years back, a Pinkerton detective had slashed his neck and severed a jugular vein. Dr. Steele and Tom had arrived just in time to ligate the vein and save his life. Bart never messed with a married woman after that.

The *Beaver*, an old double-decker, had seen better days; paint peeled away, leaving bare wood, and the sternwheel creaked with every revolution, but she made good time and churned her way through shallow water.

"Cap'n Daniels, can you take a couple passengers to St. Looee?" Tom yelled.

"Don't carry passengers no more. Oh, Tom, it is you. Sure, you can use the spare bunk in my cabin," Captain Bart shouted.

"I got a friend, but he can't pay," Tom hollered.

"If'n he cleans the pigpen, he can sleep on the hurricane deck," the captain shouted.

Zeke hauled the overstuffed carpetbag to the second deck, but Tom carried his precious instrument case. Captain Bart's cabin was a mess of empty whisky bottles and clothing thrown on the floor. "Zeke, you can start by cleaning this mess. Toss the bottles overboard and sweep the floor," Tom ordered.

The deckhands and a half-witted farm boy herded the last of the hogs up the gangway. Two large black sows stopped, sniffed the air, and, with excited squeals and grunts, trotted off toward picnic hampers carried by the Baptist Ladies Missionary Society. The dozen or so women, attired in their best high-button shoes, frilly lace, and hats decorated with flowers and clusters of artificial fruit, had just left their hired eight-passenger surreys, each drawn by two horses. It was their last outing of the year. They planned to journey upstream, admire the fall colors, sing hymns, and listen to hair-raising but satisfying stories of missionaries being stewed in a pot by unrepentant cannibals. The highlight of the trip was eating mounds of potato salad, home-cured ham, fried chicken, and a variety of pies and cakes. The ladies were teetering down the slippery landing to the small excursion steamer when the two excited pigs bowled over Mrs. Jones and proceeded to root in her picnic hamper. Other ladies dropped their picnic baskets and, with absolutely no effect, flayed the sows with their parasols. The unemployed loungers who came to watch the steamboats cheered as the deckhands rounded up the pigs, now sated with cherry pie, chocolate cake, and caramel-filled eclairs.

The *Beaver* got underway just before three o'clock. It was another warm, sunny day but time for the great migration of ducks and geese. Great flocks of ducks circled the river, looking for a safe place to roost for the night. Tom settled into a deck chair and watched as the *Beaver* churned past Horseshoe Island, where Tom and Billy had caught catfish and pickerel that they cooked over a driftwood fire. Below the island, the river opened up to a half-mile-wide shallow lake. Captain Bart steered between the channel markers.

"I ain't never been on a steamboat. Do you suppose the captain'd let me in the wheelhouse?" Zeke asked.

"Ask him, polite, and I 'spect he would welcome your company. I'll go with you," Tom said.

Captain Bart stood behind the great wooden wheel, whistling "Camptown Races" while keeping a sharp eye on the channel markers. "Hell, yes! Glad to have the boy. Might even teach him how to pilot a steamboat," the captain said.

Another boat, pushing barges upriver, came around a bend. "You, boy, pull that cord, give her two toots," the captain said. Zeke pulled the cord twice. The steam whistle sounded two long, mournful hoots that echoed off the hills back from the river.

"Two toots mean we will pass on his left side, and he has to move out of our way on account of a boat going downstream has the right of way," Captain Bart said. Sure, enough, the approaching boat turned just enough so she slid on past our left-hand side about a hundred feet away. "Another rule is that a faster boat has to overtake a slower boat on his right side. You learn the rules and the river, and maybe after ten years or so, you will be smart enough to captain a steamboat."

It was near dark when they tied up at Peoria for the night. Within minutes, the cook cried, "Come and get it!" When she had carried passengers, the dining room had been painted light blue and the table would be covered with a white cloth. Now, the bare table had greasy stains, and the room was littered with odds and ends of spare parts. The cook plunked a huge pot filled with lumps of meat, turnips, and potatoes swimming in a brownish, thick gravy. "Slumgullion stew. Take it or leave it."

A greasy, little, bug-eyed fellow, the cook glared at the crew sitting on long benches on either side of the table. "Damn, can't remember if it is horsemeat or beef. One tastes about the same as the other," he said.

Moses, the big, black coal shoveler, filled his plate with stew, and almost before the deckhands had a chance to fill their plates, he ladled up another heaping plate and went on forking down great hunks of meat smeared with brown gravy. Zeke and Captain Daniels went at the meal with great gusto, but Tom fiddled with a bit of potato and had a slice of bread. "That's enough for me. I'm going to turn in," he said.

The spare bunk was nothing more than narrow boards laid across two sea chests and covered with a straw tick. Tom stripped to his long johns and crawled in between two quilts. For the first time in many nights, he fell into a deep sleep and didn't wake until the steam engine rumbled and the sternwheel turned.

It was barely dawn when the *Beaver* backed away from the landing and headed downstream. Tom found Zeke in the dining room, chewing on thick slices of bread smeared with bacon grease, with a slice of fish fried with a coating of corn meal. "The cook put out a trot line last night, caught three nice catfish," he said. After a few bites, Tom allowed that it was about the best catfish he had ever tasted.

31

The *Beaver* boomed downriver, hastened along by the faster current. Ten miles below Peoria, they passed a huge slough teeming with ducks and geese. Tom stood in the open door to the wheelhouse with a mug of coffee. A gangling great blue heron squawked and rose from the marsh. The bird's legs dangled awkwardly, and he let loose a stream of bird shit as he rose in the air. "Down in these parts, they call those birds 'shitepokes,' and over there is Shitepoke Slough," Captain Daniels said.

The air grew warmer with each passing mile they made to the south. Tom sat out on the upper deck, soaking up sunshine and feeling his muscles and nerves loosen. The grassy riverbank slid by, and a mile or two away, steep bluffs lined the river valley. Turtles basked on logs in the morning sun but slipped off into the water as the *Beaver* churned by. A doe and a nearly grown fawn stepped daintily to the bank, drank, and faded back into the trees. A mile or so further, they passed another lake off to the side of the river. A great cloud of ducks circled, set their wings, stretched their legs, and landed on the quiet water among clumps of marsh grass. It was an idyllic scene out of an older America. Then, abruptly, clouds of smoke arose from the marsh, and a second later, booming gunfire came from the lake. Half of the great flock scrambled into the air. Some rose a few feet only to drop back with a broken wing. "Them's market hunters. Those old boys have punt guns, big as cannons, that fire a handful of birdshot and kill a dozen ducks at a time. They clean the ducks and send them packed in ice as fur away as Chicago," Captain Daniels shouted.

Zeke settled down on the deck next to Tom. "I cleaned up the kitchen and mucked out the pigpen," he said.

"I hope you did the kitchen first," Tom replied. The boy had put on weight and looked more confident.

Captain Daniels sang out, "Look there, Chautauqua Lake, and comin' up is Bell Rose Island at the mouth of Spoon River. It's shaped like the island of Cuba, so they called the town Havana. Now, ain't that somethin'." Tom shaded his eyes at a cluster of small houses in the river.

"Them's houseboats, for fishermen and hunters. Don't pay no taxes, and they can move to where the fish are bitin'," Captain Bart hollered. He gave two short toots with the steam whistle. As if in answer, a woman stepped out on the tiny porch of the last houseboat and waved. The engine slowed, then Captain Bart rang for reverse. The sternwheel churned the water until the boat just barely moved with the current. A boy in a flat-bottom skiff came out from the houseboat, rowing as hard as he could pull.

"Hey, Captain Daniels, got a mess of mallard ducks, and Ma baked four blackberry pies just for you!" the boy shouted.

"Hello, Abner. How much?" the captain asked.

"A nickel apiece for the ducks and a dollar for the pies," the boy answered.

"Here, Zeke, give him a dollar and a half for ten ducks and the pies, and here's an extry dime for the boy. Abner, tie alongside and pass up the vittles," Captain Bart shouted.

The barefoot boy with a mop of blond hair hanging down over his eyes handed up the ducks and then the pies. Zeke put the dollar bill, a silver half-dollar, and a shiny new dime in the boy's grubby paw.

"Thankee, thankee," the boy said. He untied the line, bent to the oars, and in a moment, skimmed across the river to the houseboat.

"Now, there's a born river rat," Tom said, who watched the churning wake all through the sunny afternoon. His thoughts drifted to the days in Vienna when he watched the great Billroth perform operations on the stomach that no one in America had dared to try. An entire hour went by with no thoughts about Rachel or Billy Malone, then her death came back with the familiar sense of defeat. Was he just running away from failure?

Captain Daniels broke into his black thoughts. "Tom, take the wheel. I need a little snooze." Tom gripped the great wooden, spoked wheel that required enormous attention. "Watch out for the markers; just keep her in the middle of the channel," the captain ordered.

Bart leaned back in a leather chair, crossed his hands over his chest, and was soon peacefully snoring. Tom was happy. The job took his mind away from the black torments. An hour later, Captain Bart opened one eye. "Watch out for the sandbar around the next bend," he said. Sure enough, as they rounded the bend, a long wedge of sand extended halfway across the river. Tom steered well clear, and the captain went on with his nap.

It was near dark when Captain Bart nosed the *Beaver* into the landing at a small village on the right-hand side of the river. The usual dirt road led from the landing to a cluster of shacks, a red-brick bank, and, at the end of the street, a courthouse. A three-decker steamboat painted white with gilt red trim was already at the landing, lit up like a Christmas tree. The name of the boat, in fancy black lettering on white, was *Hunt Club*. "That's a strange name for a steamboat," Tom said.

"She used to be the *Spirit of Peoria*, but her engine broke down. When she drifted onto a sandbar, a lawyer, name of Jenson, had her towed down here to Hardin. This lawyer owns the bank, the only saloon, and gives a nice bonus to the sheriff every year. He set up the *Hunt Club* for sportsmen from as far away as Chicago. There ain't no sin laws against gambling and such in Calhoun County. Rich sports booze, gamble, and have girls too. Jenson has a mint of money, and nobody crosses him, or they just might wind up in the river."

As soon as the bow stage was down and the deckhands had tied up to a couple of trees, the cook called, "Come and get it!"

Moses, the big black fireman, wore a striped shirt and a vest with a diamond stickpin. The deckhands were scrubbed clean with combed beards and spanking clean clothes. Captain Bart waltzed in wearing a dashing blue jacket with brass buttons and a string tie. The cook had roasted the ducks all afternoon. The skin was a crispy brown and the meat juicy. Each man had a whole duck; Moses and the deckhands had two. Everyone finished off the blackberry pies.

"Men, go ashore and have a good time. Young Zeke, you stay aboard, keep an eye on things. Throw a shovel of coal on the fire to keep up steam so we can get an early start in the mornin'," Captain Bart said.

Moses got up from the table, stretched, patted his belly, and took a gold toothpick out of his vest pocket. "See you fellas later. I'm goin' to see my little woman," he said.

"Moses, you done seen your little woman in Peoria last night," the cook said.

"Tha's right, but this is a different little woman," Moses said.

"Tom, let's mosey to the *Hunt Club* and see if there's a game. Just take care and watch the lawyer. Like I say, he is the law in these parts and likes to take money off steamboat men."

When the sun went down, the air turned chilly. Tom pulled up the collar of the thick tweed jacket and stood at the top of the stage with Captain Bart when an eerie cry, like a crying baby or a laughing woman, that ended in a high-pitched wail, echoed from across the river.

"God, what is that?" Tom asked.

"Oh, that's nothing but a female wampus cat, crying for a mate," Captain Bart said.

"Wampus cat? Never heard of such an animal."

"Ain't none up your way. They like warmer weather. Long ago, a hunter killed the local bobcats until there was only one lonesome, old male that mated with a barn cat and started a whole new species. The male wampus cat has a tuft of white fur on its tail, and when he dangles the end of his tail in the water, fish bite, the cat whips his tail and tosses the fish up on the bank. In the wintertime, when the slough ices over, the females sit in a circle and melt a hole in the ice with their hot breath. Then the male sticks the end of his tail in the water and, why shucks, they catch enough frozen fish to last half a year."

"That's a damn tall tale. You can't spoof me," Tom said.

Captain Bart chuckled. "Now, it just might be a tall tale, but strange things happen in these back waters. Why, some folks claim there's alligators in the river, but of course, they ain't nothing but those big gar fish."

Tom laughed. "I'll remember this story," he said.

A mahogany bar went the length of the lower deck of the *Hunt Club*, and a half dozen card tables were scattered about the center of the room. Two men were drinking and tossing down peanuts at the nearest table. One wore a badge and had a big Colt revolver in his belt holster; the other wore a handsome gray frock coat and fawn-colored trousers. His blond hair was slicked back over his collar.

"Evenin', Mr. Jenson," Captain Bart said. Jenson had slitty eyes, jowls, and a round potbelly. Along the walls and in dark corners, there were comfortable couches and big easy chairs. A mounted buffalo head with huge sweeping horns looked out over the room from the far end.

"I'm going to have a little nip of the local White Mule. What will you have?" Captain Bart asked.

"Most any kind of sody pop," Tom said.

"You a goddamned sissy?" the bartender asked.

"Don't start anything, or my boys will tear you to pieces," Captain Bart said. The bartender reached under the counter, but Captain Bart lunged across the bar and grabbed his arm. "Don't even think about going for that shotgun."

Jenson, the lawyer, put down his drink and made his way to the bar. "Luke, we don't want trouble. Give the man a root beer and pour a glass of our best Kentucky sour mash for Captain Daniels. Drinks are on the house. Welcome to the *Hunt Club*."

He gave Tom an easy smile and extended his hand. "Never seen you before. Friend of Captain Daniels?" he asked.

Tom took the lawyer's soft white hand. "Tom Slocum. I am a passenger on the *Beaver*."

"Have a good time. The drinks are on me. If you feel lucky, join us for a friendly game," the lawyer said.

Captain Daniels downed his whisky in one swallow, sighed, and put the glass back on the bar. "Wouldn't mind a little game. Tom, try your luck," he said.

Tom removed the wire from the green bottle, popped out the cork, and took a long pull of fizzy, yeasty root beer. The drink was tasty and refreshing. He quickly drained the bottle. This setup didn't look like the nickel-and-dime games he had played with medical students where, at most, he won five or six dollars. He remembered Doc Steele's advice to watch the players.

"Count me in," he said.

"Does five-card draw suit you fellows?" the lawyer asked.

"Suits me," Tom said.

Captain Bart took the chair to the left of the sheriff, who shuffled the cards, passed them to Captain Daniels, and said, "You deal."

"Ante two bits," said the captain.

Tom put two dimes and a nickel in the center of the table. Captain Daniels flipped five cards facedown to each player. The lawyer never moved a muscle, but a fleeting smile went over the sheriff's thick lips. Captain Bart made a noncommittal sigh, but Tom kept an absolutely straight face. He had a pair of eights, spades and diamonds, a jack of hearts, a six of diamonds, and a ten of hearts. He figured his best chance was to go for three of a kind or maybe two pair. He was about to trade the jack, the six, and the ten of hearts for three more cards but remembered Doc Steele had said that was a sure sign you held a pair. "I'll take two," he said.

The lawyer took one card, Captain Bart two, and the sheriff took three. "Bet a half-dollar," Captain Bart said.

Tom had drawn an eight of hearts that made three of a kind. "I'll match that and raise two bits," Tom said.

The bartender put another tumbler of whisky at Captain Bart's elbow and an opened bottle of root beer for Tom. The sheriff put seventy-five cents in the pot, but the lawyer put down his cards. "Another draw," said the captain.

Tom tossed down two cards, the captain one. The sheriff held fast. "Well, boys, are you up for another half-dollar raise?" he asked.

Tom and the captain tossed their half-dollars on the pot. "Call," said the sheriff.

Captain Bart won with three tens that beat Tom's three eights. The sheriff held two pair, queens and tens. The captain pulled in the pile of coins, picked up the cards, shuffled, and gave the cards to Tom to deal. The whisky in his glass was gone. The bartender gave him a refill. In the next two games, Tom had poor cards and folded out after the second round of bets. The root beer didn't taste quite as good as the first, and he put it aside. The lawyer won one game with a straight and another with two pair. He remained impassive. The game went on for a couple of hours. Tom won two small pots, dropped out when he had poor cards, and kept his losses low. Captain Bart scarcely looked at his cards, bet recklessly, and lost every hand. The sheriff raised his bets until every pot had a size-able stack of greenbacks. Tom kept his eyes on the impassive lawyer.

Near midnight, Captain Bart's eyes didn't focus just right and his speech was slurred. It wasn't right, Tom thought. The captain knew how to handle liquor. Tom picked up a hand. There were four spades and the deuce of hearts. The lawyer took two cards.

"Five dollars," the lawyer said.

"Three cards, and I will raise your five with another five," the sheriff said.

Tom dug into his pocket and came up with two crumpled five-dollar greenbacks. "Match the ten and give me one card," he said. He drew the jack of spades, making a straight flush, jack high.

Captain Bart didn't ask for another card but tossed in a pile of greenbacks. The betting went around to the lawyer, who took one card. "Raise twenty," he said. The sheriff and Captain Bart threw in their hands. Tom swallowed hard. The lawyer held his hand over the left side of his forehead. When he took his hand away, Tom saw a pulsating temporal artery. His face remained blank. There was no tremor, but a pulsating temporal artery meant the onset of a headache.

Tom tossed a gold twenty-dollar double eagle in the pot and absently took a gulp of root beer. The lawyer matched his bet. The root beer wasn't right. In an instant, Tom remembered a chemistry class when the students tasted chloral hydrate, a new sleeping medicine from Germany. He spit it out. "You put chloral hydrate in our drinks."

"You are mistaken. Let's see your cards," the lawyer said. Tom tossed down his straight flush. The lawyer had two of a kind; Tom pulled in the pot with over a hundred dollars. Captain Bart slumped, rested his head on the table, and snored.

"That's all. Sheriff, you should arrest the bartender for spiking our drinks," Tom said.

"Like hell. You had to cheat to win that last pot," the sheriff said.

The lawyer took a nickel-plated derringer from his vest pocket and aimed it at Tom. "He is right. Where did that last spade come from?" the lawyer snarled.

"You know damn good and well that you tried to bluff the last hand," Tom said.

"Sheriff, put these two in jail until they sober up," said the lawyer.

"I'll take my cut of the pot," the sheriff said. He drew the big Colt. "You can carry your friend."

Tom kicked his gun hand. The Colt exploded, and the bullet crashed into a bottle behind the bar. The lawyer and Tom ducked. When things came back in focus, Moses jumped into the room and smashed the sheriff with a terrific uppercut and grabbed the lawyer with his huge arm. The bartender came up with a sawed-off shotgun. Tom heaved a chair in the bartender's direction and jammed the pot of money into his coat pockets.

Moses's eyes were red, his fancy vest was gone, and the striped shirt was in shreds. "We be gittin' the hell outen of this place. There was a little ruckus uptown. When I heard the shot, I figured the Cap'n was in trouble," Moses said. The huge Negro lifted Captain Bart as gentle as if he were a baby, tucked him under one arm, and trotted back to the *Beaver*. The rest of the crew was already aboard.

"Best we get up steam and get out of here 'fore the sheriff rounds up his deputies," the cook said. Tom dragged the captain to his cabin and tucked him into his bunk, then went up to the wheelhouse. The cook, at the wheel, shouted orders while the deckhands untied the dock lines.

"What the hell are you doing? Tom asked.

39

"I been with the captain long enough to take the *Beaver* all the way to N'Orleans. See them men with the torches up by the courthouse? Them's the sheriff's posse. We best get the hell out of here," the cook said.

The posse fired a ragged volley. Bullets splintered the woodwork of the wheelhouse. Tom ducked. "Let her rip!" the cook shouted.

The engineer's distant voice came back from the tube. "Ain't got the steam."

"By damn. That kid, Zeke, was supposed to keep up fire. The little son of a bitch must have gone to sleep. Take this here bottle of kerosene and pour it on a shovel of coal to git her goin'," the cook said.

Tom ran to the engine room below decks where Moses, naked to the waist, heaved coal into the furnace, which barely showed a flame. Tom poured the bottle of kerosene onto the next shovelful of coal. The fire roared, and a blaze shot out of the open furnace door. "Dat's good. Now you, boy, help fill her up," Moses said. For the next five minutes Tom heaved shovels of coal until he thought his back would break.

"We got steam!" the engineer shouted.

Tom raced back to the wheelhouse. The *Beaver* had drifted a few feet away from the landing, but the mob waded out in the river, firing guns and waving torches. "Those sons of bitches aim to kill every one of us, lynch Moses, and set her on fire. If you know how to shoot, use that there Winchester," the cook said.

Tom aimed high over their heads. Men at the front of the mob wavered, then turned and ran. Cook pulled the cord; the steam whistle let out a blast that echoed from the bluffs across the river. The stern wheel creaked in reverse, and the *Beaver* slid into mid-river. Cook spun the wheel and the *Beaver* was off, following a moonlit path in mid-channel. When they rounded the next bend, the cook signaled for dead slow. The lazy current pushed them along, out of harm's way.

Zeke was sound asleep on the main deck between stacks of lumber. Tom kicked the boy awake. "Damn your sorry hide. Get to the galley and make a big pot of coffee," he said. The sun was over the tree line before Tom was able to arouse Captain Bart. He and Zeke poured coffee down his throat and walked him up and down the deck. They were near the Mississippi before the captain took the wheel. In a few minutes, the *Beaver* slid past the Grafton waterfront onto the broad Mississippi.

"There she is, boys, Old Saint Looie, the river queen, the biggest damn inland port in the world!" Captain Bart shouted.

Long wooden docks and landing places stretched along the river for nearly six miles. Just back of the docks stood a line of warehouses and fine buildings with signs for shipping agents. Along the docks were stacks of freight, lumber, barrels, gunny sacks filled with grain, and bales of cotton. Dozens of wagons driven by cursing draymen lumbered up streets leading from the landing to the city. Lines of black roustabouts trudged from the warehouses to the boats and back with huge loads on their backs. There were loungers, drunks, an old woman sold cigars, and bootblacks offered to clean muddy boots; girls no older than fifteen brazenly strutted along the docks, shaking tambourines and waving at the riverboatmen. Over it all was the noise of steamboat whistles and bells, the sounds of a fiddler, and the angry shouts of draymen and the roustabouts. "Why, I ain't never seen nothin' like this," Zeke said.

It was warm enough for Tom to doff his jacket and roll up his shirtsleeves. He could almost shed his misery over Rachel like a cast-off coat until he thought of how excited she would have been to see the city and the dizzying number of steamboats.

They steamed past the Anchor Line boats tied alongside Laclede's Landing. Some boats were three hundred feet long and near fifty wide; all were painted white with red and gold trim, with double stacks and side-wheels. Ladies in silk and lace with parasols and men with top hats and frock coats alighted from tasseled carriages to take passage on the great passenger boats. Black fellows, dressed fit to kill, followed the upper crust with their trunks, hampers, and leather cases. Captain Bart gave a toot on the whistle when the shabby, old *Beaver* passed the *City of New Orleans* and *The Belle of Memphis*. When they steamed past the *City of Baton Rouge* he gave a double toot and waved. "Captain Horace Bixby has that boat. Ain't she the prettiest thing you ever saw?" Captain Bart asked.

The *Beaver* nosed into a landing alongside the barges and boats that carried rough cargo, opposite a run-down warehouse with the sign Pierre Labouche: Lumber, Livestock, and Produce. Deckhands lowered the stage and made the boat fast with thick hemp ropes tied onto iron bollards.

Captain Bart, wearing his best blue serge jacket with brass buttons, marched ashore and returned with Mr. Labouche, a small, fussy man with jet-black hair slicked down with pomade. After discussing the latest news, Captain Bart led the agent to the piles of lumber on the hurricane deck. "Lookee here. Hickory for the strongest wagon spokes ever made. These oak planks will make floors for the best houses in the land. Here is a heap of black walnut boards, all cured and dry, ready for making furniture or paneling," he said.

Mr. Laclede measured the planks and scratched in a notebook. "What about the hogs?" he asked.

"Thirty head, fattened on corn. Ain't no better pork meat in the land," Captain Bart said.

The parleying went on most of the afternoon until Labouche clapped Captain Bart on the shoulders. "*Très bon! Marché conclu*," Labouche said.

"What kinda talk is that?" Zeke asked.

"That's French," Tom replied.

"That's downright un-American," Zeke said.

"The French were in these parts long before the English. Some of the towns up the Illinois River are named for the French explorers. St. Louis was French until Tom Jefferson bought the whole area from Napoleon," said Tom.

By midafternoon, roustabouts had unloaded the lumber and herded the hogs into pens. Pierre Labouche handed a wad of cash to Captain Bart Daniels, who paid off the crew and gave Zeke a silver half-dollar.

"I am as dry as the Sahara," Captain Bart cried.

"I know just the place. A good German beer will slake your thirst," Labouche replied.

"The beer is on me," the captain said.

They walked uphill from the landing to Market Place, a dusty thoroughfare lined by two- and three-story brick and wrought iron warehouses and crowded with wagons loaded with white clay, bales of cotton, and sacks of coal. Zeke's eyes bugged. "This must be the biggest town in the whole United States," he said.

"Zeke, you ain't never been to New York or even Chicago. Shucks, St. Louis doesn't hold a candle to Chicago. Ain't that right, Tom?" Captain Bart said.

"Yes, sir. There are buildings in Chicago that are ten stories high and have steam elevators so folks don't have to walk up stairs," Tom said.

They turned south to Chouteau Avenue and walked past fine brick houses with gardens and gazebos. "Best we take a street-car. I ain't up to walkin'," Captain Bart said. The horse-drawn streetcar cost ten cents and went way out to Twenty-First Street.

Schnaider's Beer Garden was next door to a brewery. Workingmen in rough overalls sat at tables under shade trees next to businessmen in suits, neckties, and bowler hats. Waiters ran from the brewery to the garden balancing huge trays with schooners of beer. Captain Daniels led the way to a table near the bandstand where a brass band blared out German tunes. "German lager costs only a nickel, and the free lunch is over there," the captain said.

Tom Slocum threw down a dime. "Zeke, have one on me, but remember, only one," he said. The light, foamy German lager was as good as he remembered from Vienna. The free lunch counter was spread with roast beef, pickles, bratwurst, rye bread, and hard-boiled eggs.

The fellows had barely dug into the free lunch counter when a trio of flashy damsels with painted faces strolled along a path between the trees. They paused when they came within range of the *Beaver's* crew and showed legs up to the knee. The engineer and two deckhands sauntered off with the ladies. Zeke nearly choked on his bratwurst. "Why, those fellows went off like they knowed those gals all their lives," he said.

"Shucks, anyone with two dollars can go with those wimin. Now, down in N'Orleans, they's girls that don't wear nothin' but red bloomers. You can play with their titties all night for a dollar," the cook said.

Tom Slocum finished off his beer and an enormous beef sandwich, then settled into a chair next to Captain Daniels. "I need to get to New Orleans," he said.

"I am going to Dubuque for a load of grain, but there are plenty of fast boats that go downriver every day," the captain said.

"Do they cost much?" Tom asked.

"Hell's fire. For twenty dollars you can have a cabin and eats all the way to N'Orleans. The *Natchez* leaves in the morning. Phineas Leathers is the captain. We call him "Old Push," on account of he don't let anyone get in his way," the captain said. He scribbled a message on a sheet of notepaper. "Phineas is an old friend. He might give you a free pass."

CHAPTER FIVE

Down the Mississippi

The *Natchez* flew the Confederate flag because Captain Phineas Leathers would not admit that the Union had won the war, even though President Andy Johnson had pardoned him for being a rebel spy. The *Natchez* had two towering, black smokestacks, an enormous red-painted sternwheel, and three decks. The pilothouse was perched between the stacks, high as a church steeple. Tom Slocum and Zeke joined the crowd of well-dressed, high-paying passengers on the stage. The mate read Captain Daniel's scribbled note and waved to a cabin boy. "Take this gentleman to the clerk."

The boy, who was at least ten years old, bowed and took Tom's carpetbag. "Foller me," he said.

The boy scampered up the wide staircase to the clerk's office on the hurricane deck. The clerk, a foppish fellow with hair slicked back from a high forehead, read the note and whistled through his teeth. "Sir, I shall take you to Captain Leathers."

They went up another wide flight of stairs. The clerk opened a door and stepped aside, motioning Slocum and Zeke to enter the grand wood-paneled pilothouse furnished with easy chairs, couches, and a gas stove with a pot of coffee. Windows on all four sides gave a view of the river, St. Louis, and miles of Illinois farmland across the river beyond East St. Louis. The splendid, highly polished, wooden wheel stood in the exact center of the room directly behind a window. Speaking tubes, levers, pull ropes, and all the appurtenances required to steer the great boat were within easy reach.

The clerk touched his cap and almost kneeled before Captain Leathers, who lounged in an easy chair. Mississippi steamboat captains were lords of the universe, the right hand of God, who could burn holes in lowly civilians with a single glance. The captain had a full beard flecked with gray and was resplendent in a blue suit with gold buttons that would have done justice to an admiral of the Royal Navy. "Damn you, boy. I am conferring with my pilots," growled the captain.

"Sir, this note is addressed to you, personally," the clerk said. The captain adjusted his spectacles and read out loud.

> *My dear Old Friend, Captain Leathers,*
> *The bearer of this note, Dr. Tom Slocum, saved my life after a damned Pinkerton detective slashed my throat. The good doctor is on a mission of mercy and is in a hurry to reach New Orleans. I know you will give him every courtesy and speed him on his way.*
> *Yours, respectfully,*
> *Bart Daniels, Captain of the Beaver*

Captain Leathers boomed like a Baptist minister. "Mission of mercy? If you are a friend of Black Bart, likely you are up to no good. That damn pirate was on Grant's side at Vicksburg, but he knows steamboating. What in Sam Hill are you up to?" asked the captain.

"Sir, I am off to Indian territory to find my best friend who is missing in action against the Apaches," Tom said.

"Likely to get yourself killed by them murderin' savages. You a medical doctor?"

"Yes, sir," Tom replied.

"Always need a doctor when the damn passengers get to shootin' and stabbin' one another. Clerk, put him up in a good cabin."

The salon, near the whole length of the hurricane deck, was over two hundred feet long but only thirty wide. Tom and Zeke gawked at chandeliers with gas lights, intricate carvings over the doors, Turkish carpets, brass spittoons, card tables, couches with soft cushions, and upholstered chairs. An ornate mirror stretched behind a grand mahogany bar at one end of the room.

46

Early arrivals were at ease on chairs and couches, sipping coffee or early morning toddies.

The first-class passenger cabins ran the length of the salon, set back in porch-like recesses off the outer passageway. The clerk bowed and gestured toward an ornate door beneath a carved lintel. "Your stateroom, gentlemen," said the clerk. The room was furnished with two bunks, two chairs, and a basin of water on a small table. An ornate rug adorned the floor.

Zeke plunked down on a bunk. "Why, this is the softest mattress I ever seen," he said. The cabin boy set the instrument case and carpetbag by the door and held out his hand. Tom gave him a nickel.

The steam whistle blew, the steam engine revved up, and the sternwheel churned up muddy water. The *Natchez* eased away from the dock, gathered speed, and within an hour they were hightailing it downriver.

A steward rang a bell. "Dinner time! Dinner ti-ime!" he shouted. Stewards unfolded long tables, set up cane-bottomed chairs, flung white cloths on the tables, lit candles, and, within moments, converted the salon into an elegant dining room. Tom and Zeke joined thirty men at the first table. Tom sat next to a middle-aged gentleman, who, by the looks of his black frock coat, cravat, and pince-nez spectacles, appeared to be a professional man. The fellow had a round medal, the size of a silver dollar, with *De Viridire* engraved beneath a horse with a rider brandishing a saber.

"Colonel Leander Cleburne, lately of the Alabama Volunteers," he said.

"I am honored," Tom said.

The colonel thumped a square-cut glass, filled to the brim with a tawny beverage, on the table. "Rye whisky and Peychaud's bitters with a dash of absinthe, finest remedy for the grouches, fevers, sore throats, and bad-colored piss that mortal man ever made," he said.

"Which of those ailments are you suffering with?" Tom asked.

A steward flung a platter of beefsteaks on the table, and another put down a whole roast turkey with a long carving knife and fork. Colonel Cleburne sniffed. "Pshaw, I am fit as a fiddle, just an excuse to drink these newfangled cocktails."

Other men at the table snorted, laughed, dug into steaks, and helped themselves to dishes of creamed peas and heaps of boiled potatoes. Zeke cut a thick slice of turkey and poured on a ladle of gravy. The men grew raucous, while, at the next table, entire families, including uncles and ancient grandfathers, did their best to keep children from racing up and down the long salon and flinging food at one another. Further aft, a flock of mothers and daughters, fresh from shopping trips in St. Louis, maintained decorum. When it didn't seem possible to eat another bite, the stewards brought lemon, pecan, and cherry pies. Zeke managed a slice of all three. The men lit up seegars and called for brandy. Stewards, as if by magic, folded the long dinner tables and brought small marble-topped tables fitted out for games of chance.

"Zeke, I aim to increase my winnings. This ain't no place for a young fellow. Go on and get some sleep," Tom said.

"Aw, shucks, I ain't hardly sleepy."

Tom crossed his arms over the back of a chair and sipped a sarsaparilla. The bemedaled colonel took his place at a table with three young planters who had sold their cotton crop in St. Louis. Cleburne flicked a lavender-colored handkerchief from his cuff and patted his lips.

"Sambo, a deck of cards and drinks all around," he said.

A bright-eyed fellow pulled a silver cigar case from an inner pocket of his elegant fawn-colored coat. "Sir, you wear the highest Confederate medal. I would be honored if you would accept a Hoyo de Monterrey," he said

The colonel touched the silver medal. "I humbly accept your kind offer, although I prefer a Davidoff. Bobby Lee presented me with this medal after Gettysburg. We have not been introduced. I am Leander Cleburne, former colonel of Alabama Volunteers," he said.

"I am most honored, sir. I am Raphael Macron, at your service. My late father also served in the great cause."

The other men introduced themselves as the cards and drinks arrived. The bartender caught the colonel's silver dollar in midair. "Thank you, Sambo," Leander Cleburne said.

Cleburne opened the new deck, shuffled, then passed the cards to Raphael, who cut the deck and passed it back. "Is seven-card stud satisfactory?" Cleburne asked.

"Fine, fine with me," the trio of young planters said. Cleburne dealt a down card then one faceup to each player. Macron bet five dollars. The others passed until the next round, when Macron bet ten dollars. The others stayed; each put greenbacks in the pot. Cleburne's next faceup cards were a deuce and a nine of hearts. Macron had a king of spades and a queen of diamonds showing. The betting went around until Macron took a hundred-dollar pot with a king-high straight.

Tom Slocum watched but had no inclination to join the high-stakes game. Leander Cleburne gradually increased his winnings, often with one lucky card. At least once each game, he removed his flouncy lavender handkerchief from his cuff to dab his lips, clean his spectacles, or to touch the medal, as if to draw attention to his former heroics. When the youngest player, a callow, fuzz-faced, elegantly dressed stripling, yawned and threw in his hand, Tom could not resist the temptation. "Mind if I join you? I am Dr. Tom Slocum."

"Welcome, Doctor, though, by your accent, you are not a Southerner. Sambo, a drink for the doctor," Cleburne cried. Cleburne was friendlier with the bartender, most likely an ex-slave, than one would expect from an ex-Confederate officer. The game, seven-card stud, went on as before. Tom had good down cards, bluffed his way through two hands, and doubled his money within a half hour.

Cleburne waved his handkerchief to Sambo. "Another drink and a new deck," he said.

Macron dealt. The betting began. Tom had bad cards, folded, and dropped out but kept his eyes on Cleburne, who bet, raised, and bet again. The third young man, well into his cups, piled gold eagles and greenbacks on the table. Cleburne's face cards showed two aces, diamonds and hearts. "Call," he said. Cleburne won when the ace of spades in the down pile made three of a kind, ace high.

Tom Slocum pocketed his winnings. "That is enough for me. Hard to play when the new deck has an extra ace of spades.

You slipped it from the bottom of the deck up your sleeve along with that handkerchief," Tom said.

Macron snatched a nickel-plated revolver from an inside pocket. "No damn Yankee cur can accuse a Southern gentleman of cheating," he said.

Tom slid off his chair and dove beneath the table just as Macron pulled the trigger. The bullet plowed a furrow in the Turkish rug. Few players looked up from their dice or cards at the sound of the gunshot, but one portly gentleman with flowing white hair, a white goatee, and a matching white suit, aided by a thin black cane, tottered to his feet. "Gentlemen, I am the honorable Reginald Fitzpatrick, judge of the highest court in the state of Alabama. Ladies are present. We must have no gunplay or foul language," he said.

"This damn Yankee insulted Leander Cleburne, a former officer in the Confederate Army!" Macron shouted.

The judge staggered closer and peered into Cleburne's face. His visage took on a dull purple cast as if he were about to fall into an apoplectic fit. He touched the silver medal with the tip of his slender, black cane. "Leander Cleburne fell at the Battle of Charlottesville. This man is an imposter."

With his words still ringing, he slashed his cane across Cleburne's face. Sambo fairly leaped from behind the bar and swept the pile of greenbacks, twenty-dollar gold eagles, and silver dollars into a large sack that he closed with a drawstring. He then took the imposter under his mighty arm and bounded for the door. In an instant the two leaped over the railing into the swirling waters of the Mississippi. When last seen, they were swimming vigorously toward Missouri. Tom carefully turned each card on the table faceup. There were, indeed, two aces of spades. Macron slumped in his chair. "My apologies," he said.

Tom had scarcely sunk into the luxury of a feather mattress when he woke to loud banging on the door. "Doctor, come quick."

Tom came out of a deep slumber. "Wait just one damn minute," he said.

The door burst open. A mate swung a lantern in his face. "Man is going to bleed to death 'fore you getcher ass outen that bed," he said. Tom pulled on pants and shoes, grabbed the instrument case, and followed the mate to the main deck. He stumbled over passengers on the deck who curled up amongst bales of cotton. They grumbled, turned over, and went back to sleep. Up forward, behind the engine room, a gang of firemen surrounded a huge, red-haired hulk of a man stretched out flat in a pool of blood. He had an ugly slash that went from his cheek, under an ear, and to the back of his head. The engine made a terrible racket, pistons roared back and forth, and the deck vibrated so it was hard to stand upright.

"Take him to the salon. Put him on a table where there is light," Slocum said. It took four men to heave the patient up the stairs and lay him on a table beneath a gaslight. The card players hardly looked up from their game while Slocum washed away sooty dirt and poured a solution of carbolic acid into the wound.

"Who did this?" Tom asked.

"One of them goddamn German deckhands." The speaker had an Irish accent.

Tom tied ligatures around spurting arteries, then stitched the wound and repaired the left ear. "By Gar, he looks better than ever," said a sooty-faced fireman.

The red-haired giant hurled himself off the table, crashed against the flimsy wall, and, with a right hook, felled one of his friends. The scuffle continued until a mate with a belaying pin waded into the battle. Tom packed his instruments and went out on deck.

The *Natchez* roared along. Sparks shot from her twin stacks; the searchlight lit up the river a half mile ahead. The wooded bank, sandbars, and the great muddy river slid past. Just after dawn, the old pioneer town Saint Genevieve, a mile or so back from the river, came into view. A little after noon, the *Natchez* pulled into the long dock at Cairo to take on crates of chickens and coal, then she thundered off on the mingling waters of the clear-blue Ohio and the muddy Mississippi.

51

At Memphis, roustabouts carried sacks of grain to warehouses along the waterfront and returned, rolling barrels of Tennessee whisky over the cobblestones. "If the river went dry, we could float all the way to New Orleans on whisky," Tom said.

The *Belle of Calhoun*, a brand-new side-wheeler, docked next to the *Natchez* and unloaded bales of cotton. Her captain strutted high on her Texas deck. "Captain Leathers, you old billy goat! A thousand dollars says I will beat you to New Orleans!" the *Belle*'s captain shouted.

Captain Leathers shook his fist. "You damned whippersnapper! The *Natchez* is the fastest boat on the river. By God, I'll take your money."

The *Natchez* got underway first and thundered down the river, a half mile ahead, before the *Belle of Calhoun* left the dock. Pilots kept a lookout for snags and sandbars while another took the wheel. Captain Leathers paced up and down the Texas deck with his eye riveted on the *Belle of Calhoun*. The *Belle* sounded her whistle three times, and great clouds of black smoke and sparks belched from her twin stacks.

"She's a-gainin." Captain Leathers shook his fist. "An extry day's pay and drinks for all hands!" he shouted.

The furnaces roared, the engines created a furious din, and the decks vibrated so a person could hardly stand upright. The *Natchez* lead decreased by a whole boat length, and near midnight, the engineer reported that the boilers were red hot. The firemen paused, drank a ration of whisky, and let the boilers cool. The betting odds changed when the *Belle of Calhoun* gave a mighty blast of her steam whistle. Flames, instead of sparks, flew from her stacks.

"What in tarnation? The damn fool must be pouring oil on the coal!" Captain Leathers shouted. Two hours later, the *Belle* was less than a hundred yards behind. Ladies in their nightgowns emerged from their cabins to see the show. Yard by yard, the *Belle* crept up on the *Natchez* until she was close enough for passengers to shout insults across the water. Just before the break of dawn the *Belle* was alongside, no more than fifty feet away. Captain Leathers ordered more steam, and the *Natchez* drew half a boat length ahead.

The two great steamboats hurtled down the river, neck and neck. Whisky-swigging passengers clung to rails and gaped at the opposing boat. Tom Slocum and Zeke leaned far out over the railing. "Ain't this more fun than a horse race at the county fair!" Tom shouted.

Flames roared skyward from the *Belle of Calhoun's* stacks and she surged ahead; muddy water boiled in her wake. The *Belle* was about to overtake the *Natchez* when a terrific explosion erupted from her boiler room. The blast vaporized the upper decks and pilothouse and threw red-hot metal, arms, legs, decapitated heads, and flaming bits of wood a hundred feet into the air. Passengers ran from the flames when fires broke out on the top deck of the *Natchez*. The *Belle* disintegrated, but passengers at the bow and stern hung on until they were flung into the muddy waters, where they were in danger of being sucked under by giant whirlpools left as the *Belle* went under. Crew and passengers of the *Natchez* threw anything that would float to the victims. Zeke, without a word, kicked off his shoes, dove overboard, and swam to a man furiously paddling and trying to support a child. Captain Leathers stopped the engines and ordered boats to pick up the struggling survivors. Zeke returned with the spluttering man and a half-drowned child, then stroked his way to another victim. The salon quickly became a gruesome, makeshift hospital.

Tom's first patient had been caught in super-heated steam from the exploding boiler. Slocum removed the victim's clothing, but skin came away with the shirt and pants, leaving an anatomical display of muscle, tendon, and bone. The poor soul took one last, strangling breath and died. Slocum set broken bones, smeared carbolated Vaseline on burned flesh, and bound wounds. Patients howled with pain after his supplies of ether and morphine were exhausted.

Tom could not bring himself to work without anesthesia on the mangled leg of a piteous boy; he searched his instrument case and found a bare half ounce of chloroform. Throughout the long hours, he had scarcely noticed a young woman with sleeves rolled to her elbows making bandages cut from strips of gowns and women's underclothing.

"I can give anesthesia," she said. The woman put the boy to sleep with a few drops of chloroform. Tom washed the wound, pushed the splintered tibia into position, and sutured a flap of skin over the dreadful wound, then applied a splint.

"I can barely feel his pulse!" the woman cried. Tom tied the last knot to hold the splint in place. He found a weak beat in the carotid artery, then nothing. The child was deathly pale, his lips were blue, and his eyes stared into nothingness. Tom sensed a great emptiness, put his head in his hands, and thought he should give up surgery, but he blazed with anger.

"You gave too damn much chloroform!" He instantly regretted his outburst; there hadn't been enough chloroform left in the bottle to harm a fly. The woman slumped over the dead child; her tears turned a smudge of blood on her cheeks into pink rivulets.

"You have a right to be angry. He was beyond help. You did a fine job," she said.

"How would you know?"

"My father is a surgeon. I assist him at the Touro Infirmary," she said. She opened her arms and welcomed Tom to an embrace fueled by fatigue, sadness, and despair. She closed the boy's eyes, covered his body with a blanket, and her lips moved in silent prayer. Tom, for the first time, noticed her black, curly hair and soft gray eyes. He had paid no attention to another woman since he was first with Rachel, but his wife had never worn jewelry. This woman had a sparkling gold necklace with a six-sided star.

"That is an unusual necklace," said Tom.

"It is the Star of David that signifies God's protection."

Tom said, "God did not protect this boy or any of these people."

"For us Jews, it means spiritual protection," she said "I am Ruth Herschel. If you are in New Orleans, visit my father, Simon," she said.

The groans and shrieks of the pitiful survivors cast a pall over the *Natchez*. Tom Slocum and Ruth Herschel did their utmost to relieve the suffering. There was no morphine, but there was plenty of whisky and brandy. At Vicksburg and Baton Rouge, volunteers carried the injured to hospitals and the dead to makeshift mortuaries.

CHAPTER SIX

New Orleans

S teamboats lined the docks at the Port of New Orleans as far as the eye could see. Ocean-going steamers and full-rigged sailing ships from all over the world plied the harbor. The news of the disaster had flown down the river by telegraph. Darkened carriages and horse-drawn hearses met the *Natchez* at the foot of Canal Street.

The bedraggled man was too weak to carry the boy Zeke had saved. Zeke swung the child up on his shoulder and carried him to the wharf. The boy's father directed him to an elegant four-horse carriage. His plantation supervisor removed his hat and bowed.

"We were worried about your safety," he said.

"This young man saved our lives. Give him one hundred dollars," the fellow said.

The supervisor pulled a large purse from his waistcoat pocket and counted out five gold double eagles. "Here you are," he said.

Zeke jingled his handful of gold coins. "Thank you, sir. I ain't never seen this much money," he said.

Tom Slocum steadied Ruth Herschel's elbow when they descended the stage and walked to an open barouche driven by an elderly black man. "Where are you staying?" she asked.

"A friend recommended the Bourbon-Orleans Hotel."

"Watch out. It is haunted by children who died in a yellow fever epidemic," she said.

"Come now, you can't believe in ghosts," he said.

"This is New Orleans. We bury our dead above ground. Their spirits are free to roam," she said.

"I must replenish my supplies of medicines. Where is a good pharmacy?" he asked.

"My father can help you." She held Tom's hand a moment longer than necessary. "Jesse will meet you tomorrow and take you to the hospital. Will nine be satisfactory?" she asked.

"Fine," he said. The old black man gently helped her into the carriage and drove off. Tom watched them depart with an ache in his heart.

"Let's walk to the hotel; Ruth said it is up Chartres Street, past the cathedral," Tom said.

"I ain't never seen so many different kinds of people," Zeke said. Peddlers pushed little wagons, hawking trinkets, cheap watches, and pencils. Negros, whites, and people every shade in between, along with friars in long robes, and fashionable ladies swirled through the crowd. Women sold vegetables, flowers, and fruit while men in bloody aprons hacked at carcasses and laid slabs of beef and pork on tables.

"I can't understand a word they say," said Zeke.

"Some of it is French and Spanish, the rest is Creole, a mixture of French and African. Let's have coffee," said Tom. The café au lait, with milk, sugar, and chicory, was nothing like either of them had ever tasted.

Zeke bit into a pastry covered with powdered sugar. "Ain't this sumthin'. Say, look at them pretty girls. I aim to get a new suit of duds and go lookin' for that gal in the red bloomers," he said. Tom finished his coffee.

"Well, damned if there's old Andy Jackson on a horse," Zeke said.

"He whupped the British in eighteen twelve," Tom said.

Zeke stopped before a dry goods store with men's suits on display in the window. "Ain't them the grandest duds you ever seen? I'm gonna have me a pair of them striped pants," he said. They passed brick buildings painted in light blue, pink, or green. Galleries half enclosed with iron railings and filigreed curlicues hung out over brick sidewalks. "Why, New Orleans must be the greatest city in the whole world."

The lobby of the Bourbon-Orleans was filled with tables, sofas, and huge vases of flowers scattered among fluted marble columns. Gentlemen lounged on easy chairs, smoking and reading newspapers. The desk clerk sniffed. "Are you country boys in the right place?" he asked.

Tom slapped down a twenty-dollar gold piece. "We want a room with a balcony that looks over the street, for two nights," he said.

The room was pleasant, and the gallery gave a fine view of throngs of people who walked with a languid Southern air. When they had settled, Tom sipped a lemonade and enjoyed the street scene. "I'm gonna git me a new set of duds and have some fun. Mebbe I'll find that gal with the red bloomers," Zeke said.

"Stay out of trouble," Tom replied.

In the morning, Zeke had not returned when Dr. Herschel's barouche arrived. "G'mornin', sir. I'se takin' you all to the Touro Infirmary," a grizzled, elderly Negro said.

Tom extended his hand. "I am Dr. Tom Slocum."

"Well, sir, I am Jesse, been with Dr. Herschel goin' on twenty years."

They set off toward the river on St. Peter's Street, then drove past fine old buildings, mansions set in wide lawns surrounded by trees. "Tell me about the Touro Infirmary," Tom said.

"Oh, the infirmary is a fine place, mighty fine. They takes care of all folks, just like old Judah Touro said when he gave the money. They got the best doctors in N'Orleans," Jesse said. In less than half an hour, Jesse turned from Louisiana to Foucher Street and jogged through rows of shade trees where relatives pushed patients in wheelchairs. Others were on benches scattered through the park that spread before the handsome three-story stone building.

Tom alighted from the carriage, awestruck by the grand front entrance with fluted columns. Ruth Herschel, wearing a long white dress with short sleeves and a high collar, met him in the lobby.

"Dr. Slocum, meet my father."

Dr. Herschel, an aristocratic man of perhaps fifty years, had a goatee streaked with gray. "Ruth has told me of your splendid surgery," he said.

Tom was struck by the doctor's old-world manners and appearance, reminiscent of Viennese doctors. "You are most kind. I am looking forward to seeing your work," Tom said.

"I will be operating on a man with a strangulating rupture," Dr. Herschel said. Tom could not believe his good fortune. Few surgeons, even in Europe, had dared to operate on ruptures or hernias. Most doctors tried to push the gut back into the abdomen with brute pressure.

The operating room was spotlessly clean, and Tom, along with the nurses and Dr. Herschel, changed into a clean white shirt and trouser, a system recently introduced by German surgeons. The patient, a dock worker whose hernia bulged from his lower abdomen, rapidly went under the ether anesthesia. Dr. Herschel and Ruth scrubbed their hands and arms and then dipped into a carbolic solution. Ruth assisted her father to make a long incision in the man's groin over the bulging mass of intestine. She clipped and tied bleeding vessels as skillfully as any surgeon. "I attended classes at the Tulane Medical School, but the professors refused to allow me to take the anatomy course," she said.

Dr. Herschel gently squeezed the intestine into the abdomen and stitched the hernia. "That was beautifully done," Tom said.

"Thank you. Now we shall visit the ward patients," the doctor replied. It was an enjoyable afternoon, but Tom couldn't make up his mind about Ruth. She was confident, self-assured, and knew more about medicine and surgery than most doctors.

It was late afternoon when they parted in the lobby. "Dr. Slocum, New Orleans is growing. We could use more well-trained surgeons. Consider returning when you have finished your mission," Dr. Herschel said.

Tom blushed, "Thank you, sir. I shall remember that."

Ruth Herschel smiled but said nothing. Tom felt a pang of regret and remembered their embrace. He thought of returning to this idyllic city and a fine practice, or was he thinking of a life with this woman?

"I must find the Southern Pacific station and a place to replenish my medical supplies," he said.

"The station office is at 227 St. Charles Street, and La Pharmacie Française is only a short distance away. Jesse will take you there," Dr. Herschel said.

Signs in the ticket office announced two trains a day to California. The Sunset Express left that night. Tom approached the barred window. "I am going to the Arizona Territory. Two tickets for tonight's train, please," Tom said.

"You get off at Lordsburg. Train leaves at eleven thirty, sharp," the agent said. Tom bought two first-class tickets and took a cab to the hotel, hoping to find Zeke.

The boy had a black eye, dried blood beneath his nose, and vomit stains on his pink shirt and striped pants. Tom yanked him out of bed. "Ezekiel, damn your hide, where in Sam Hill have you been?"

Zeke groaned and touched his tender eye. "Oh God, it started so fine, then that big fella busted me up," Zeke said.

"Pull yourself together. We leave on the night train and must get supplies," Tom said.

"I paid twenty-five dollars for these striped pants and a pink shirt and a fine, blue checked coat. I told the clerk I wanted to find the girl who wore nothin' but red bloomers. The fellow snapped his suspenders like he knew her. 'Shucks, she lives down on Basin Street in the big fine house with marble columns out front. Just ask for Miss Lulu White. She knows all those girls,' the clerk said."

Tom threw Zeke a soaking wet towel. "Clean your face and scrape the rubbish off your clothes."

Zeke rubbed away the blood and perked up. "I found the place, just like he said. A big black man let me in the front door. You ain't never seen such a room. There were mirrors on every wall and big gas lamps and chandeliers that lit up the place just like it was daylight. I asked for Miss Lulu White. The big black fella pointed to a little bitty, black-haired woman who was sittin' on a gold chair. She looked me over like I was a piece of meat. 'What do you want, boy?' she asked. 'I'm a lookin' for the girl in the red bloomers.' I said. 'You got enough money for one of my girls?' I showed her three double eagles and a half dozen silver dollars. 'My, ain't you a rich young man? Mary had to go see her sick mother, but you can meet her friends.' I was a mite disappointed until she rang a little bell. Before you could say 'scat,' a bunch of pretty girls sashayed into the room. They wiggled and pranced 'til my eyes just about bugged out. After I swollered a couple of times, I pointed to a pretty blonde-headed girl who wore nothin' but black stockings and a lacey thing that hung down almost to her legs. She had titties like big ripe peaches. She giggled and took me to her room on the third floor. Durned if she didn't flop down on a great big bed and wriggle her finger. 'Won't you be more comfortable without all those clothes?' she asked. I left on my long johns and went to kissin'. I was playin' with her titties, and things just got better and better. 'That will be five dollars. How long do you want to stay?' she asked. 'I want to stay with you fer all my life,' I answered. She giggled and we went at it again. After a while, she ordered a drink called a Hurricane, that tasted sweet and just fine. I had another and then felt swoony in my head and got sick. That was when the big black man gave me a couple whacks and tossed me out the door. I din't wake up 'til daylight and din't have no money or my new coat," Zeke said.

"You are lucky to be alive, and you might have caught a disease from that girl," Tom said.

"Somethin' like a fever or the trots?" Zeke asked.

"Worse than that. One makes your privates swell up, and it hurts to piss so bad you wish you were dead. The French pox starts with a red sore, then goes to your brain so you can't walk, think, or see straight."

Zeke rocked back in forth on the bed. "I asked her if the frilly little bit of lace was a petticoat. She said it was a camysole and come from Paris. Ain't that in France?" Zeke cried.

"It sure is," Tom replied.

"Oh, God, I'll get that French pox for sure."

"Come on, you can carry the supplies," Tom said.

La Pharmacie Française had everything Tom needed. He looked longingly at surgical instruments imported from Europe, but after buying more ether, chloroform, and carbolic acid, his money was almost gone. "You might consider this new drug from Germany, called cocaine, that cures a lot of ills and works as a local anesthetic in the eye and on wounds," the clerk said.

One drop of the cocaine made Tom's mouth numb. "Amazing. I will take a bottle," he said.

CHAPTER SEVEN
The Sunset Limited to Lordsburg

Low-hanging clouds spit rain when the hack left Tom and Zeke off at the station. "Lookee at that engine," Zeke said. The huge Baldwin four-four-zero engine, painted black with red wheels, chuffed and puffed billows of black smoke over Canal Street.

"Stop gawking and don't let go of our bags," Tom said.

Slocum carried the instrument case and a satchel with his new supplies. A porter with a round, smiling face touched his shoulder. "Your tickets, gentlemens?" He peered at the tickets. "Destination, Lordsburg. Car four, seat ten, gentlemens; ah will fetch your bags. You just foller me," the porter said.

"Thank you, George," Tom replied.

"How'd you know his name?" Zeke asked.

"All porters are nicknamed 'George' after George Pullman, who invented the sleeping car," Tom said.

Oil lamps suspended from the ceiling cast a cheerful glow over the paneled, first-class carriage. George led Tom and Zeke to their seats, which were already turned down for sleeping. "Gentlemens, heah is your place, with blankets and a pillow for each of you," he said.

"The advertisement said there would be sheets and a pillowcase," Tom said.

"Oh, dat be extry," George said. Tom flipped a silver half-dollar. A big smile split George's face. "Yes, sir. Sheets and pillowcases for the gentlemens. The men's room is thataway," he said, pointing to the end of the car.

Zeke sunk and was snoring in the upper bunk before Tom had removed his shoes and settled in for a night's rest. Tom could not shake away memories of the nights he had shared with Rachel, but then Ruth Herschel crept into the edges of his thoughts. He was bone-tired but wide awake when the train's whistle shrieked into the night. The engine chuffed; the car jerked, stopped, then jerked forward again. Tom peered out the window. The train rolled through the center of the city, then past backyards of smaller houses, and finally by the outlying shacks until city lights gave way to the black dark of a cloudy night. Tom rested his head on the pillow and listened to the clickety-clack of the rails as the train gathered speed. Sleepers groaned, snored, and rolled to find a comfortable spot. At the far end of the car, a woman hushed a crying baby.

Tom had drifted into a troubled doze when the train's shrieking whistle roused him. Clouds and rain had given way to bright moonlight and a vista of water, trees, and occasional houses on stilts next to canals. The train slowed and jerked to a halt next to a small station. The murmur of musical French voices greeted alighting passengers.

It was full daylight when the Sunset Limited stopped for coal and water at Lafayette. Tom rolled out of his bunk, rubbed his eyes, and decided to stretch his legs on the platform. A push-cart vendor called, "Café au lay, café au lay, hot beans and rice."

Tom gave the leathery-skinned fellow a two-bit piece for a mug of milky coffee, which he finished just before George shouted, "All aboard!"

The endless, low swampland gave way to higher ground, with glimpses of elegant buildings set in groves of oak and pine trees and surrounded by fields of cotton. Zeke pressed his face to the window. "This country's big and so different. I figured it all looked like Pa's farm in Illinois," he said.

When they crossed the Sabine River, a tall fellow with a big hat passed a bottle. "We done left them Coonass Cajuns; we is now in God's country!" he shouted.

The landscape changed to rolling hills with dense forests interspersed with grasslands and cattle ranches. In midafternoon, the whistle shrieked, the train slowed and ground to a halt while a half dozen men on horses, wearing big hats and boots, drove a herd of longhorn cattle across the tracks. Zeke opened the window to wave at the cowboys, but billows of black smoke and dust poured into the car.

"Shut that damned window!" a thick voice shouted.

Zeke coughed and slammed down the window. "I was just wavin'. Them cowboys have a swell life," he said.

They followed the twisty Brazos River into Houston and clanked to a halt at the new Union Station to take on coal and water and let the passengers stroll the platform. "You fellers from out of town?" the station agent asked.

"We come all the way from Illinois," Zeke said.

"You come to the right place. Houston is booming, gonna be the biggest city in the whole country afore long," the clerk said.

"We goin' to Injun country to fight Geronimo," Zeke said.

"You fellas must be plumb crazy. Them savages done whupped the whole army and kilt half the white people in Arizony. You boys best stay right here and get rich like everyone else."

The train whistle blew. "Time to get back," Tom said.

The train passed herds of longhorn cattle, ranch houses, and more cowboys on horseback. There were also clusters of adobe huts with dark-skinned men wearing derby hats and colorful blankets flung over their shoulders. They stopped long enough in San Antonio to get a glimpse of the Alamo.

"That's where Davy Crockett fought the Mexicans," Tom said.

"I'll bet he kilt 'em all," Zeke said.

"No, the Mexicans killed every man in the Alamo, including Crockett," Tom replied.

"Are you foolin' me? Davy Crockett coulda won with one hand tied behind his back," Zeke said.

"He ran out of gunpowder and food," Tom said.

"Well, that explains it," Zeke sighed.

The land changed to dry desert, enormous red rocks and low hills with only an occasional adobe hut. It appeared to be wild, empty, and inhospitable. Was this a wild-goose chase? How could he find Billy in this huge, empty desert? Tom's thoughts drifted to Ruth Herschel and her father's suggestion that he stay in New Orleans. Was the surgeon merely being polite, or did he mean it? Then, as clear as day, he saw in his mind's eye his son, Daniel. How could he have gone off and left the boy? Was he happy? Did his aunt tuck him into bed every night?

A new porter made up the beds, but Tom watched the landscape go by until it was dead dark.

CHAPTER EIGHT

Lordsburg

The train halted, lurched ahead, and after a moment, the conductor cried, "Lordsburg, Lordsbuurrg, the train stops in Lordsburg for one hour!" Tom rubbed his eyes, pulled on his clothes, and looked for Zeke. The boy was already hauling Tom's bag down the aisle. As usual, Tom carried the instrument case. The air was crisp and chilly. A stinging wind drove clouds of dust from a corral with dozens of kicking and whinnying horses next to the depot. Half a hundred long-horned cattle in another pen added to the noise, dust, and general ruckus. Men wearing broad-brimmed hats, faded blue shirts, and wool pants tucked into knee-high boots toted sacks and barrels from an open boxcar on a siding to two double wagons with teams of twelve mules. A grizzled black man with the gold chevrons of an army sergeant bellowed at the work detail.

"Them black fellows must be buffalo soldiers," Zeke said.

Tom rubbed the dust out of his eyes and squinted against the rising sun at the saloons, a hotel, a couple of cafés, and an all-purpose mercantile store along a sandy street. Shacks and tents were scattered on the other side of the tracks, but beyond the stores were a sizable number of respectable-looking wood and adobe houses. Horses were tied to hitching posts outside the cafés and the saloons. Every man carried at least one revolver in a belt holster and horses at the hitching posts had Winchesters in saddle scabbards.

"I need to make some inquiries. Might as well start with Mary's place," Tom said. The menu tacked on the wall behind the counter read Beefsteak, Eggs, and Biskits, Forty Cents.

A hard-faced, red-haired woman slung two mugs on the table and poured coffee. "You gents want breakfast?"

"I guess we will have the special. Are you Mary?" Tom asked.

"Yeah, what of it?" Mary answered.

"Who might know where I can find an old army friend?" Tom asked.

"Go find Tom Horn, biggest frog in the pond; works for the army," she said.

"Thank you, ma'am." The beefsteaks were big but took a lot of chewing, the eggs were greasy, but the biscuits were fine. Tom finished his coffee and left two bits on the table.

Tom Horn leaned against a hitching post, chewing a toothpick. Horn was over six feet tall and two hundred pounds of solid muscle. He wore a broad-brimmed felt hat, an army blue shirt, and a long-barreled revolver in a hip holster. He wasn't any older than Tom Slocum, but his face was weathered and almost as dark as the buffalo soldiers struggling with a wooden case at the open door of the boxcar.

"Don't you bastards drop that ammunition!" Tom Horn shouted over the wind. "You gents looking for work?"

"I am looking for my friend, an army lieutenant. The war department sent a telegram to his folks, claimed he was lost in action in the Arizona Territory," Tom Slocum replied.

Tom Horn took his time while he fixed a cold glare on Dr. Slocum, then looked at the soldiers loading wooden cases onto the wagons. "Damn you, lazy bastards! The guns and ammunition go in the second wagon!" Horn yelled at the soldiers. "I am taking supplies to Fort Bowie. If you have questions about a missing soldier, talk to an officer on General Crook's staff. As soon as we get these wagons loaded we are headin' that way. Can either of you shoot or drive cattle?"

"I kin herd most any animal, but I ain't got no horse or saddle," Zeke said.

"If you are any damn good, I will give you three dollars to herd cattle from here to Fort Bowie. Sergeant Blake will fix you with gear," Tom Horn said. He fixed his ice-cold gaze on Slocum. "What the hell are you?"

"I'm a doctor," Slocum said.

Horn spit a gob of tobacco on the fire. "Can you dig out bullets, treat snakebite, fix busted bones, and sew scalps back on?"

"I can do all of that," Dr. Slocum answered.

"Then git on the first wagon."

Sergeant Abner Blake had been a field slave before the War of the Rebellion, who joined the army to fight Indians instead of picking cotton. At six feet and barrel-chested, he could lick any man or beast who crossed his path. He mopped his face with a bandanna, pushed his hat back on his head, and jerked his thumb at Zeke. "How in hell am I supposed to fight murderin' savages with another goddamn greenhorn? You skinny little sonabitch probably don't know the hind end of a cow from a Chicago whore," the sergeant growled.

"I kin herd cattle or horses or alligators as well as any man," Zeke said.

"Is that so? Kin you herd those animals when the Apaches are taking potshots at you?" Blake asked.

"Damn right," Zeke replied.

"Pick your gear and take any cow pony out of the herd that suits you," Blake said. Zeke took a worn McClellan saddle, a blanket, a nose bag, and a thimble with a lariat to tether the horse. He cut a sassy gray mare out of the half-wild herd. When he settled the horse with sweet talk and a double handful of oats, he put a blanket on her back, folded the skirts and girth over the seat, and with his left hand on the pommel and his right on the cantle, he heaved the saddle on her back and tightened the girths.

"Pretty good for a greenhorn. Better take a carbine too," Sergeant Blake said.

The cook served up beans and scalding hot coffee at noon, and an hour later, Tom Horn got astride his big stallion and waved his arm. "Get 'em started!" he shouted. He put spurs to his horse and cantered off to the southwest. A Sharps buffalo rifle hung in a scabbard in front of his saddle, and a Winchester .44-40 carbine was tied to the saddle's pommel.

"You expecting trouble?" Slocum asked.

"In these parts, trouble is waiting in the next gully," Horn replied.

A dozen buffalo soldiers surrounded the wagons, while as many cowboys and drovers got the horses and cattle moving. Tom Slocum heaved his instrument case and bag onto the first wagon and settled on the wooden seat next to the driver.

The bullwhacker, a wiry fellow with a huge Mexican sombrero tilted back on his head, cracked a whip over the mules. "Get along, ye damn good-for-nothing, lazy bastids!" he yelled. The lead mule perked his ears, and after another crack of the long whip, the team moved out on a dim, winding trail that went across a barren landscape of short, tan grass, low brush, and outcrops of yellow rock. Tom shaded his eyes and looked at a line of hazy, snaggle-toothed, blue mountains rising from the plain like an island in the sea.

After the mules started, the bullwhacker turned to Slocum. "Howdy. Call me Pete. Ain't got no other name. Pa didn't leave no name and no address. Ma calls my little brother Re-Pete. Ain't that the damndest thing?"

"I'm Tom Slocum, glad to meet you. How long to Fort Bowie?"

"Depends on the damn Apaches. Might take five days, probably longer if we meet up with a bunch of the murderin' savages," Pete said.

"Why can't the army control a few Indians?" Tom asked.

"Hellfire and damnation. You folks back East don't understand. The Apaches ain't just one tribe, they's a whole bunch of different bands. Old Geronimo has mebbe fifty men and twice that many women and children, then there's Naiche and Mangas Coloradas and Victorio. The army can't ketch the bastids on account they don't stay in one place but roam as far south as the Sonora Mountains in Old Mexico."

"Can't the army track them down?"

"Hell, they don't leave no tracks. They gits up on the rocks, and in a minute, they disappear like a wisp of smoke. They don't have no reglar place to live on account of they make a livin' by huntin' and stealin' and tradin' with the Mexkins."

"How do they survive in this godforsaken desert?" Tom asked.

"Hell's fire! This here grass is good for deer and antelope, and there's bear and wild sheep in the mountains. The Injuns eat plants and roots. Those mountains up yonder are the Cheery-cow-wahs [Chiricahuas], where they live part of the year," Pete said.

The sun was a huge red ball on the western horizon when Tom Horn galloped back. "Make camp by Willow Creek!" he shouted. A half hour later, the wagons reached a clump of cottonwood trees by a narrow stream of clear water. Tom Slocum was so dry he could spit dust. He ran to the stream, fell flat, and doused his head in the cool water, then sucked up a drink. It was dark by the time the horses and cattle had drank their fill at the stream and settled into the meadow of good grass. Dinner was beefsteak and beans with coffee. Tom Slocum sat with the men around the cooking fire. Small animals made rustling noises among the trees, frogs chirped, a coyote howled, a lost calf brayed for his mother, and snatches of song came from the night riders keeping watch over the cattle and horses.

"You got a weapon?" Tom Horn asked.

"A cap-and-ball, thirty-one caliber Colt," Dr. Slocum answered.

"Pretty damn useless," Horn replied.

"A friend carried it at Shiloh," Slocum said.

"Takes a lot more power to knock down one of these Indians. They are the toughest, meanest men that live on this earth."

"I don't aim to kill no one. I came out here to find my best friend," Slocum said.

"When those Apaches come, it's either kill or be killed," Pete said.

Tom Slocum stared into the dying fire and drained the last of his coffee. "Mr. Horn, what brought you out west?" he asked.

Horn sat on his haunches. His features were lost in the shadows. "I left the farm in Missouri when Pa whipped me until I couldn't walk. If I had stayed, I would have killed him. What about this friend you are looking for?" Horn asked.

"Billy Malone was the strongest boy, the best shot in Sandy Ford. Once, he broke up a Ku Klux Klan meeting with a slingshot. He could light fires, track animals, and was smart too. The newspaper editor knew the governor and got him into West Point."

"If the Apaches caught him, they might have sold him to the Mexkins. You better learn the lingo." Tom Horn pulled a worn notebook from his vest pocket. "Most Apaches speak some Spanish. This here has enough words to get you by," he said. The notebook had columns of English, Spanish, and Apache words.

One by one, the buffalo soldiers rolled up in their blankets and drifted off to sleep. Tom Slocum stirred the fire and threw on more kindling. "What are the chances we will run into Apaches between here and the fort?" he asked.

"We probably won't see hide nor hair of an Indian. Ain't many of them left. This used to be Cochise's stronghold when he was chief of the Cheery-cow-wahs. He was friendly with the Americans until the army chased his people to the San Carlos Reservation. The braves got bored, drank homemade beer, and broke out of the reservation a year or so ago," Horn said. He drew a map in the sand. "We are about here, up ahead is the north end of the Cabeza Mountains, then beyond the next valley are the Cheery-cow-wah Mountains. Tomorrow we meet up with the old overland trail. The Butterfield stagecoaches went this way until the railroad came through. Cochise's son Naiche might have a small band in these parts, but most likely he is with Geronimo down in Mexico."

They broke camp before daylight and had cold beans, johnnycake, and coffee for breakfast. Pete rounded up his mules, hitched the harnesses, and, with a string of blue curses, got them in the traces.

"Fill your canteens; it's a long way to the next water hole!" Tom Horn shouted. The wagon lurched forward after Pete cracked his whip and threatened the mules with everlasting damnation. All the long day, the wagon swayed, bumped, and rocked over the boulder-strewn trail. At noon, Slocum got out and walked. They drew deeper into a range of hills, gullies, and small canyons. The first water hole was bone-dry, and it was well after dark before they found a spring with a pool of water.

The next morning, they passed heaps of rocks and a pile of adobe bricks. "What happened here?" Tom asked.

Pete leaned to one side and spit a stream of tobacco juice. "Them's graves. Was in Sixty, mebbe Sixty-One, an Apache raidin' party burned down the station, killed all the stage passengers, and stole the horses." He pointed at a nearby hill. "Usta be a ranch up there. Them savages killed the rancher, the hands, the wife, 'n' took a little boy. Folks say he grew up Apache."

The wagons lurched along for another mile past juniper, mesquite, and dry grass. "Up ahead is Doubtful Canyon," Pete said.

"How come it's doubtful?" Slocum asked.

"Well, sir, back when I drove stagecoaches, it was just plumb doubtful that we would make it through the canyon on account of the Apaches lay behind the rocks to ambush the coach."

Before noon on the third day, the trail went uphill through the east end of the Animas Valley. "See, that hill over there is Stein's Peak. The Apaches usta keep lookouts up there," Pete said. The wagons were well into a small valley between hills covered with reddish boulders and tall rocky columns. Tom Horn rode a quarter mile ahead of the strung-out wagons, horses, and cattle. A ragged volley of rifle shots erupted from the hills. Tom Horn turned, whipped his horse, and raced back to the wagons with bullets zipping into the trail on both sides.

"Dismount! Take cover!" he shouted. Indians rose up from behind boulders on both sides of the trail and fired. Two soldiers dropped like sacks of potatoes. The rest scrambled under the wagons.

Pete dropped the reins and grabbed a double-barreled shotgun. "Git under the wagon, ya damn fool," he said. Tom Slocum leaped down and crawled beneath the wagon behind a wheel just as more warriors on horseback rushed from behind. "Them bastids are Naiche's people!" Pete yelled.

A half dozen Indians, led by a tall, handsome Indian with shoulder-length hair, galloped out from behind the rocks and stampeded the horses and cattle. The cowboys and soldiers dove behind rocks and poured bullets into the racing Indians, who guided their horses with their legs and fired at the soldiers. Two painted savages rode out of the dust and gun smoke to the second wagon, grabbed the harnesses of the mule team, and, with loud yipping and shouting, got the wagon moving down the trail and up a side canyon. An Indian wearing nothing but a breechclout, a feather in his shoulder-length hair, and a quiver of arrows across his back came no more than twenty feet from Tom Slocum. A broad white stripe of paint from his forehead, down his nose, and on to his lower jaw split his dark face. He gripped his horse with bare legs and, with one fluid motion, released a half dozen arrows in as many seconds. Two struck soldiers, and another thunked into the ground next to a wagon wheel. Pete fired both barrels. The load of buckshot smashed into the Indian's right arm and knocked him from his horse. The skirmish lasted no more than ten minutes before the Indians dashed out of range. The downed Indian got up on his knees, blood streaming from wounds. The right arm dangled at a crooked angle. Tom Horn came from the firing line, unsheathed a long knife, grabbed the Indian's hair, and bent back his head. The Indian boy spit at Horn, who drew back the wicked knife, intent on taking off the boy's head.

"No, no, he is only a boy!" Slocum shouted.

Tom Horn had a look of cold anger. "Keep out of this, damn sawbones," he said.

"He is wounded and a prisoner. Don't you have any common decency?" Slocum asked.

"He is old enough to kill white men," Horn said.

Slocum stood by the wounded Indian and leveled his empty Colt at Horn. "Leave him be," Slocum said.

Horn sheathed his knife. "He's going to die anyway."

The wounded Indian fell back into a pool of blood.

Two soldiers were dead and more wounded. Slocum arranged instruments, bandages, and bottles of carbolic on the top of a barrel and had the wounded troopers put on a rough plank table. He gave chloroform, cleaned the wounds, cut away dead tissue, and removed steel-tipped arrows and lead bullets. When the troopers were put to rest in the wagon, he checked the Indian boy, who was in the dirt where he fell. He was no more than fourteen or fifteen years old but was hard-muscled. When Slocum felt for a pulse, the boy opened one eye and stared at Slocum with a look of pure hatred.

"*Indaa ligande*," he said.

The boy kicked Tom's knee. "That will larn ya. Called you white-skinned," Pete said.

"Put him on the table," Slocum said. The wounds were covered with dried blood and dirt. The load of buckshot had torn through the biceps muscle and fractured the upper arm bone between the shoulder and elbow. Jagged bone splinters protruded from the wound. The slugs had plowed a jagged gash across the boy's breast, leaving ragged muscle and a bare rib. The boy gritted his teeth and struggled. He would not let Tom touch him until troopers held him while Tom held a rag soaked with chloroform over his face. It took nearly an hour to clean the wound with carbolic, remove splinters of bone, and stitch the long gash over his chest. The ragged ends of the fractured humerus were separated by pieces of muscle, but the nerves and artery were intact. Slocum jammed the ends of the bone together with all his strength and held the arm against the chest with bandages soaked in antiseptic. It was the best he could do. If the wound became infected, the arm would have to come off.

"We ain't puttin' no damn Indian in the wagon," Horn said. Tom settled the Indian boy on a pallet of blankets next to the wagon.

Zeke came into the camp with the cowboys. "We done lost half the herd. I expected once we started shootin', the savages would turn and run. I figured I hit at least two of them, but they never stopped. It's like they ain't human. They had repeatin' rifles and fired ten shots to our one," Zeke said.

In the evening, Tom eased the men's pain with whisky and laudanum, but there was hardly enough water. The wounded troopers were feverish and thirsty. The Indian boy leaned against a wagon wheel but kept a watchful eye on the soldiers. Tom consulted Horn's notebook for the right words. He pointed to the boy's injured arm. "*Da Nzho* [It is good]," Tom said.

Tom held a cup of water to his lips. "*Tu* [water]." The boy tried to brush the cup away with his good hand. Tom put the cup to his lips again. This time, the boy took a sip, then, while Tom tipped the cup, he drank.

"*I nituwe he* [Who are you]?" Tom asked.

There was a long silence.

"*Yanuza*," the boy finally said.

"Damn waste of time. He will run away when it gets dark," Pete said.

Tom covered him with a blanket and, most of the night, tended the wounded troopers. The boy was still there in the morning. At breakfast, Pete put a plate of beans on his lap. "Mebbe he will be a tame Indian," he said. The troopers rigged a travois made of poles and strips of rawhide that they dragged behind a horse for the boy. They rounded up the stray horses and cattle and got underway by midmorning. Tom Horn found the stolen wagon in a side gully. The mules and guns were gone and the wagon smashed.

"It was Naiche's band. They got away with fifty new Winchesters and a thousand rounds of ammunition. There will be hell to pay," Horn said. The Indians didn't attack again, and except for smoke signals in the mountains, there were no signs of the Chiricahuas. The wagon bumped and swayed over the rough trail.

"I kin help you with the lingo, since I got me a tame Apache woman who cooks good and takes care of the young uns," Pete said. Tom practiced Apache words but could not get through to Yanuza.

The boy gained strength, and by the third day after his injury he managed to ride a horse. Horn tied his legs and hitched the horse to the wagon. "Ain't no more water till we gits to Apache Spring," Horn said.

The rough trail led higher into the mountains, where the low brush changed to oak and juniper trees. "This here was all Cochise's country until the army whipped him 'bout ten, twelve years ago," Pete said.

The springs bubbled up in a rocky basin shaded by trees, then trickled down a steep ravine. Red-headed woodpeckers flitted through the trees, and animal tracks surrounded the pool. It hardly looked like a battleground. Tom Slocum rested in the cool air beneath a tree, and even Yanuza drank his fill of water and seemed more at ease.

CHAPTER NINE

Fort Bowie

The wagon train came through a shallow canyon and up a steep hill to Fort Bowie, which overlooked a spring of clear, cold water. Buildings were grouped in a square around an open field in front of a low mountain. Bugle calls sounded, and a troop of soldiers drilled on the parade ground. A half mile from the fort, there was a cluster of teepees and huts made of branches covered with animal hides, with the hair on the outside. Women pounded grain in stone bowls or tended pots over cooking fires. Young boys played a game with long sticks and a hoop, and old men sat on their haunches, smoking and talking.

"Them's tame Indians, families of the Apache scouts," Pete said.

"Are they on our side?" Tom asked.

"Some of the tribes hate each other more than they hate us 'Mericans. They kin track most anything that walks on feet. Without them scouts, the army would be blind as bats," Pete said.

Zeke and the cowboys herded the horses and cattle into the stables and corrals. Pete drew the wagon up to the quartermaster's warehouse so the soldiers could unload sacks of flour, sugar, and barrels of salt pork. "Where is the hospital?" Tom asked.

"Way over, outside the parade ground," Pete said.

The hospital was a fairly new clapboard building with windows on all sides. Just inside the front door, a hospital steward smelling of whisky lounged with his feet up on a desk. A wooden examining table and a cabinet with bandages and instruments were behind the desk, and in the next room, sick soldiers lay on wooden cots.

"I need to talk with your doctor about my wounded men and a badly wounded Indian boy," Tom said. The steward scratched his belly.

"Ain't got no doctor. We got beds for your wounded soldiers, but the Indian belongs in jail," the steward replied.

"He deserves treatment, same as any other human. I will speak with your commanding officer," Slocum said.

The steward's bloodshot eyes flickered at Slocum's outburst. "I spect you kin talk with the general's adjutant, but he won't give a damn," the hospital steward said.

The adjutant's office was in a neat building a long walk across the parade ground. A sergeant, stiffly at attention on the porch, barred Slocum with his carbine. "I want to speak with the adjutant about my wounded men and an Indian boy," Slocum said.

"Lieutenant Neal is busy," the sergeant said.

"I will see him or go to the commanding officer," Slocum said.

Without a word, the man did an about-face, entered the office, and, within minutes, returned. "The lieutenant will see you now."

Neal was a slender, half-bald man of about forty behind a desk littered with paper and a scattering of copper pistol cartridges. He rubbed his eyes as if he had just woken from a sound sleep. He wore a spick-and-span blue uniform with brass buttons, and a rope of gold braid hung from his right shoulder. The walls of the office were bare except for a map of the Arizona Territory and northern Mexico. He frowned and shuffled papers.

"Who the hell are you?" Neal asked.

"Doctor Tom Slocum. I came with the wagon train that was ambushed. There are wounded men, but there is no doctor at the hospital," Slocum said.

"You a real doctor? Not some quack from back East?" Neal asked.

"I graduated from Rush College in Chicago and studied at Edinburgh and Vienna."

"Then what in tarnation are you doing in this godforsaken place?" Neal asked.

"I am looking for Lieutenant William Malone, who was reported missing in action."

"Malone was a damn fool, went missing on a patrol in Mexico. I expect he is dead."

"I intend to find him," Slocum replied.

"Can't let a damn civilian wander around by himself," Neal said.

"I will search until I find him, dead or alive," Slocum replied.

Neal tapped a pencil on the desk and twisted in his chair. "You can damn well get on the next train going east," Neal said.

"The newspapers in Illinois will hear of this," Slocum said.

Neal shrugged his shoulders. "You better talk to General Crook."

While he trudged across the parade ground, Tom remembered General Crook's heroic reputation. Crook had been wounded and was taken prisoner by the Confederates during the War of Rebellion. After the war, he trounced the dastardly Sioux and Cheyenne Indians, who had murdered Custer. General Sherman said Crook was the greatest Indian fighter in the US Army. Now he was commander of the Arizona Territory to once and for all subdue the Apaches.

The commanding officer's house was behind the officer's quarters on a gentle slope that led up to a small mountain. There wasn't a tree in sight, only low brush and clumps of dry grass. The three-story house was sided with clapboards, the roof was shingled, and there was white trim around the windows. It could have been a home in any midwestern town but was out of place in these barren mountains. Slocum stood, uncertainly, at the foot of the steps leading to the front porch. A fellow with bushy sidewhiskers that curled down his chin and out from each cheek reclined on a wooden chair with his head down on his chest. He wore rough jeans, a butternut shirt, and a ragged coat, more like a farmer than an army officer. Slocum hesitated. "Where can I find General Crook?"

The fellow on the porch raised his head. "I am General Crook. Pray, who are you and what do you want?"

"Sir, sorry to bother you. I am Dr. Tom Slocum. My friend Lieutenant William Malone is missing in action. I intend to find him."

The general sighed. "Yes, Malone was a brave man and an excellent officer, got along with the Apache scouts, and even learned the language."

"What happened to him?" Slocum asked.

"Geronimo and his band left the reservation back in June, rode into Mexico. Malone, with Troop A of the Sixth Cavalry, commanded by Captain Crawford, rode into the Sierra Madre Mountains. The troop followed Geronimo and his band until they ran out of food and their horses wore out. Folks back East don't understand how hard it is to find these Apaches," the general said.

"But where is Lieutenant Malone?" Slocum asked.

"He went up a hidden canyon with the scouts, but the Apaches ambushed the party. The scouts claimed the Apaches killed Malone, but the troopers didn't find his body. Animals most likely finished off his carcass. Crawford claims Mexican militia was in the area too. The army did all it could to find him. You can't do any more, and besides, this ain't no place for a civilian," the general said.

"I already been in a fight and cared for wounded men," Slocum said.

"You a medical doctor?" the general asked.

"Yes."

"You want to know what happened to our last surgeon?"

"Tell me," Slocum replied.

"He was with Crawford on the same mission. The Indians captured the doctor, stripped him naked, staked him out flat on his back, and cut away his eyelids. He stared at the sun all day while the ants and flies chewed on him. The poor man went blind and died the next day," the general said.

Slocum felt a sudden chill. "If you are up to the job, I will hire you as a contract surgeon. A hundred dollars a month and rations," the general said.

"I'll take the job," Slocum said.

The hospital steward sobered up after Tom locked up the whisky and laudanum. He then ordered beef broth and iron tonic for the wounded men. Within a week, they were up and ready for duty. The Indian boy, Yanuza, refused medicine and wouldn't eat the hospital rations. At the end of a week, his eyes were sunken and his flesh had wasted away. His wounds were mending, but Slocum was afraid he might die from starvation.

Slocum was changing dressings and cleaning wounds on a chilly morning when Pete arrived with a red swelling on his jaw like a dead ripe peach. "Hurts, somthin' awful, can't hardly eat nothin'," he whispered through clenched teeth.

"It's an abscess. Got to pull a tooth," Tom said.

"God, it will hurt worse," Pete moaned.

"Sit in this chair and lean your head back. Won't take a minute," Slocum said.

Jake, the hospital steward, gleefully put a fearful collection of forceps, a mallet, a thin pry bar, and chisels on the table. Slocum poured a tablespoon of chloroform on a wad of cotton and held it over Pete's nose. "Take a few deep breaths," Tom said.

Pete held his breath after the first whiff, then coughed, breathed, and went to sleep. Slocum pried open his jaw with a wooden plug. The next-to-the-last molar was rotten and broken near the gumline. Slocum couldn't get a good hold with the forceps. "Damn it all. Give me the hammer and a blunt chisel. Hold his head steady," Slocum said. He held the chisel at the gumline and whacked it with the mallet. The tooth didn't loosen. Pete moaned but settled after another dose of chloroform. Slocum pried upward on the rotten molar until it came loose and came out with a tug on the forceps. Thick yellow pus drained from the socket.

"Wake up, you old fool. It is all over," Slocum said.

"You ain't even started yet," Pete said.

"Get yourself in that bed, and we will fix a hot bran poultice for your jaw," Slocum replied.

The swelling went down, and after two days, Pete demanded beefsteak and johnnycake for breakfast. "By God, I will find a nice young squaw to warm your bed," he said.

"I would rather know the whereabouts of Lieutenant Malone. Have you heard any news?" Slocum said.

"Ain't no news. The damn savages cut all the telegraph wires. Crawford and Davis are down in Mexico with half the army, but they can't find old Geronimo," Pete said.

"Damn it all, Crook beat the Indians up north. What is so different here?" Slocum asked.

"These Apaches hide and move fast. The Mexicans pay a hundred pesos for Apache scalps, but they can't find them either. Last I heard, the renegades came back across the border to steal horses and cattle. They killed at least twenty ranchers. President Cleveland is raising holy hell with Crook," Pete said.

"The Indian boy won't eat. I am afraid he will die," Slocum said.

"There is a woman in the village, name of Das-Te-Sah, who claims to be a healer and speaks some English. Take him to her," Pete said.

Yanuza perked up when he saw Indian boys practicing with bows and arrows and the younger ones playing the hoop and stick game. Women dressed in ankle-length skirts, with babies strapped on their backs, stirred pots of food over fires, and young girls prepared animal skins for clothing. Pete guided Tom and the Indian boy to the village and asked the whereabouts of the woman healer. A squaw motioned to a crude brush hut more than a hundred yards away, all by itself. The woman, Das-Te-Sah, held a bandanna over her face.

"I have heard that you heal with plants and roots," Slocum said.

She turned her face to one side and answered in English. "I have powers to heal," Das-Te-Sah said.

"Can you help this boy?" Slocum asked.

"I might help him," she said.

Slocum removed the dressings from the boy's chest. The long gash had healed, leaving a red scar. He left the board splints and bandages on the broken arm. The Indian woman noisily sucked in her breath. "It is good. You are also a healer," she said.

She stretched her arms to Yanuza and dropped the bandanna from over her face. Her nose was split in half, from the tip halfway to her forehead. Her face was hideous. Slocum recoiled in disgust, but with professional curiosity, he touched her nose. "What happened"? he asked

"I slept with another man. My husband did this to punish me," she said.

With more optimism than he felt, Slocum said impulsively, "I can fix your nose."

She snatched up the bandanna and held it to her face, "No, impossible," she said.

"You have nothing to lose. If the operation fails, it cannot be any worse. I will speak to the general about using the hospital this very night," Tom said.

A private let Slocum into the general's sparsely furnished living room, which was lit with a double oil lamp on a table between Crook and his wife, a white-haired lady with a sweet smile. The general blew fragrant clouds of pipe smoke, and Mrs. Crook had a pile of knitting on her lap.

"Sir, I have an unusual request. There is an Indian woman in the village with a split nose. She is a good woman and a cousin to Geronimo. I can repair it with an operation but must use the hospital."

Crook threw the *Tucson Weekly Citizen* to the floor and aimed the stem of his pipe at Slocum. "Damn newspaper says I am soft on the Indians. The governor called for my resignation. What will they say if you mollycoddle a damn squaw?"

"Now, George, it won't hurt to help the poor woman. Kindness might help to bring them back to the reservation," Mrs. Crook said.

"Damn if you might be right, Mary. You better not kill the woman, or there will be hell to pay," the general said.

Tom Slocum honed his scalpel to a fine edge, soaked his instruments and strands of hair from a horse's tail in a solution of carbolic. The horsetail sutures were finer than any made of silk or linen and, when threaded on the smallest sewing needle, would not leave stitch marks. The problem was how to give

ether and operate on Das-Te-Sah's nose at the same time. He
had thought about the operation through a sleepless night and
wondered if it was too much for a country surgeon.

The thermometer stood at a few degrees below freezing,
but the split-nosed woman walked from the village and across
the parade ground to the hospital without a coat. She wore her
usual soft moccasins, a ragged but colorful Mexican blouse, and
a striped, cotton, ankle-length skirt. Yanuza walked at her side
wearing an open buckskin vest that showed a long scar across
his chest. He held his head high, and his stride was that of a
warrior, not a boy. He scowled at jeering soldiers.

Tom met them on the hospital's porch, nodded a greeting,
and gestured for the woman and boy to enter the treatment
room. "You will lie on the table," he said. Das-Te-Sah, without
a word, gathered her skirt, climbed on the table, and placed her
hands across her breasts.

"Tell Yanuza to sit in the corner," Slocum said.

The split-nosed woman spoke to Yanuza, who refused to
move away from the woman. "Tell him if he doesn't go to the
corner, I will have the soldiers put him in jail," Slocum said. She
spoke again, with authority in her voice. Yanuza squatted and
remained silent, but there was fire in his eyes.

"Jake, scrub your hands and rinse in the carbolic." Slocum's
order was sharp. Jake, without his usual whiny complaint, vigorously scrubbed with a brush and yellow soap. Slocum adjusted a
thick pad of cotton over her nose and poured on a few drops of
ether. She breathed the fumes, coughed, and tried to brush aside
the pad. Slocum waited a few moments and poured more ether
until Das-Te-Sah was deeply asleep. "The straight scalpel," he
said. Jake gave him the sharp knife, wooden handle first. Slocum made the first cut through scar tissue. Blood spurted from
an artery. Yanuza stood, his eyes hot with anger; he uttered a
sound that was half hiss and half growl. Slocum paused for a
moment, pointed the scalpel at Yanuza, and with all the power
he could muster, spoke in English. "Down." He lowered the
knife and cut away more scar tissue on the other side of the
notched nose. Yanuza never took his eyes off the woman. When

her breathing became more rapid, Slocum stopped cutting and poured more ether. When he was satisfied that the raw edges of skin and cartilage were clean and free from scar, he passed the threaded needles from one side of the V-shaped incision to the other. The work was tedious, but after a dozen stitches, the sides of the nose came together.

"God almighty, Doc, it looks good," Jake said.

It really does look good, Slocum thought. He applied bandages and stepped away from the table, exhausted by the work. It was a half hour before Das-Te-Sah came out of the deep anesthesia. She vomited, choked, and would have rolled off the table, but Yanuza caught her with his good arm. They helped her to a cot. She vomited again but gradually came awake. Her hand flew to her face. She felt the bandages and uttered a guttural cry. Yanuza soothed her with Apache words. Two hours later, she rose from the cot, adjusted her skirts, and, without a word, walked to the door, down the porch, across the parade ground, and back to her crude wickiup with Yanuza at her side.

When he wasn't taking care of wounded soldiers, Tom Slocum asked troopers for news of Billy Malone. Most said the missing lieutenant was dead. He learned enough Apache and Spanish to talk with the Indian scouts. There was no news of his lost friend, but some claimed the Mexicans took Anglos for ransom.

Slocum went to the Indian village on the first day of January. Das-Te-Sah was beside a small cooking fire in front of her wickiup. Women and children peeked and giggled, but when he removed the bandages, they cried out with great excitement. The wound had healed, and her face was almost normal. Slocum snipped out the stitches and gave Das-Te-Sah a small hand mirror. "Oh, oh!" she cried.

Yanuza glanced from the woman to Slocum, said nothing, but his expression softened. The women and children crowded closer, gabbling and laughing. One woman touched Das-Te-Sah's face. "It is good," she said.

Yanuza proudly described the medicine that causes deep sleep and the operation in great detail. The women welcomed

Das-Te-Sah back into the band with feasting and dancing that went on into the night. Pete and his Apache wife sat next to Slocum, close to the great fire. "They claim you have great power," Pete said.

CHAPTER TEN

Captain Crawford

Captain Crawford led his men into the fort just before dusk on the coldest day in January. The captain's head drooped low, and he just barely held the reins of his horse. The troopers swayed on their mounts, and some clutched the pommels of the saddle to keep from falling. They were gaunt, unshaven, their clothing was in tatters; some had pieces of blanket tied around their feet in place of boots. The scrawny horses were in even worse condition, and the half dozen pack mules were no better. One horse collapsed, leaving his rider sprawled in the dust just at the gate. Soldiers ran to help and brought a half dozen of the twenty-odd men to the hospital. The fit, clean Apache scouts, looking far better than the soldiers, raced off to their teepees and wickiups. Their wives and children ran to meet them with shouts of joy.

Dr. Slocum and the hospital steward cleaned septic wounds, set broken bones, and tended to the starved, half-delirious soldiers until after midnight. In the morning, the wounded were able to take soup and coffee. In the full light of morning, Tom operated on a steel arrow point lodged in the hip joint of a young buffalo soldier. The boy coughed and choked on the ether, but after a ten-minute struggle, he went under enough for Tom to make an incision and follow the arrow's tract deep through muscle until he could grasp the point with rat-toothed forceps. He pulled with all his might, but the barbed steel point was lodged in bone and didn't budge. He chiseled away bone around the point and tried again. It came out with a gush of bright red blood from an artery deep in the wound.

"Damn, oh, damn. I can't find it," Tom said.

"I cain't find a pulse, and he is pretty pale," the steward said.

88

Tom packed the wound with half a yard of gauze and pressed with all his might. The bleeding stopped, and the boy slowly came awake. Tom sat at the desk, head in hands. This was another of those failures that, like a black cat, had followed him since Rachel's death.

He asked the injured men for news of Billy Malone. The troopers, with a far-away look in their eyes, would only mumble about the ambush. One sergeant, a graybeard with a broken arm, had known Lieutenant Malone. "Better you talk to the captain," he said.

Tom Slocum found Captain Emmett Crawford in his quarters just after taps. The room was severely furnished, with a camp cot, two straight chairs, and a desk. A small fire crackling in an iron potbellied stove took the chill out of the air. The fort was quiet except for low voices and an occasional peal of laughter from the nearby officer's mess.

"Sir, I am Dr. Tom Slocum, a contract surgeon. May I speak with you for a moment?"

Crawford was in his early forties, had been wounded at the Battle of Spotsylvania during the late war between the states, and had the gaunt, melancholy look of a man who had seen too much blood lost in battle. His comrades claimed he never drank and was honest, brave, and modest. The Indians called him the "Tall Captain" and respected his decency. When he had been in charge of the reservation, he treated the Indians well and had protected them from crooked traders. Crawford was Crook's right-hand man, charged with bringing the renegade Apaches, especially Geronimo, back to the reservation.

Crawford put down his iron pen and shoved a stack of papers to a far corner of his desk. He drummed his fingers against the plain pine and ran his hand over his sun-darkened face. "Perhaps another time," Slocum said.

"Oh no, this is as good a time as any. How can I help you?" Crawford asked.

"I came to find my friend, Lieutenant William Malone. I understand he was under your command when he went missing. Could he be alive?" Slocum asked.

Crawford straightened in his chair, but the military bearing quickly gave way, and he slouched forward as if he was weary beyond all endurance. "Yes, I knew him well, very well, in fact. Malone was one of the few officers who made friends with the Apache scouts and spoke enough of their language to make jokes. He dressed like them and learned their ways. We followed Geronimo and Naiche to their winter camping grounds near Casa Grande. They left no tracks, but the scouts saw a wisp of smoke and tethered horses over a ridge. I thought it was their camp, but when I attacked at dawn, the Apaches had left. Lieutenant Malone volunteered to take a dozen scouts into a canyon to hunt them down. The scouts say he was a half mile or so ahead when they heard shots. Malone did not return, and the scouts could not find him," Crawford said.

"Did they ever find his body?" Slocum asked.

Crawford rubbed his eyes. "No, no body. There was a smear of blood, but no body. It was as if he had disappeared into thin air. Even if a wolf or a mountain lion had gotten to him, something would have been left."

"He could still be alive," Slocum said.

"There were Mexicans about. They hate both the Apaches and Americans and may have thought Malone was a scout. Lieutenant Malone had upset a rich Mexican rancher when he made inquiries about a child of one of our scouts. They had their reasons for killing him."

"Could the Mexicans or the Apaches have taken him alive?" asked Tom.

"The Mexicans usually make captured Americans slaves and then demand a ransom. He could be in a Mexican jail, but more likely held in slavery if he is alive," Crawford said.

"He could be alive."

"I doubt that Malone is alive. He didn't have a chance against Geronimo's men. The Indians left a false trail and disappeared like smoke. They know all the water holes in the high mountains and can live for weeks on a bag of dried meat and roots. The Mexicans trade repeating rifles and ammunition for horses and cattle. We have single-shot rifles, so in a pitched battle, they have the advantage of more firepower. Geronimo is supposed to have supernatural powers that protect him from bullets, and he can predict future events. His followers are devoted to him. I followed him two hundred miles into the Sierra Madre Mountains in Mexico but never found him. I doubt that he has Malone," Crawford said.

"Who are the scouts?" Slocum asked.

"Good Indians, gave up fighting to protect their wives and children. They live on the reservation and have taken the white man's way. The Apaches are not all one tribe. The Mimbreños, Bedonkohe, and Chihene mostly live on the reservations, but the men get bored, drink homemade beer, and beat their women or go off on a raid. Geronimo is a Chiricahua, but he married a Bedonkohe woman, so her family follows him. Cochise was once chief of the Chiricahua, but he was killed ten years ago. Naiche—his son—and Geronimo lead the Chiricahua band. The reservation Apaches are afraid of the renegades because Geronimo and Naiche steal women. We give the scouts a rifle, ammunition, food rations, a blue shirt, white trousers, and a red headband so we know they are our men. They are happy to chase renegades like Geronimo and Naiche."

"I want to go on the next patrol," Slocum said.

"No, you are a civilian. This is an army matter. If Malone is still alive, it is our job to find him," Crawford said.

"Those wounded men should have had medical attention long before they came back. How many of your men died who could have been saved by a doctor?" Slocum asked.

Crawford slouched lower in his chair. "You heard what the Apaches did to our last doctor. I can't allow a civilian to go on patrol."

"Then I will go alone and hunt for him," Slocum said.

"That is even worse. We have permission from the Mexican government to go after the Apaches, but many Mexicans think we are invading their land. They will kill you on sight."

"I will find a way," Slocum said.

"If you are so determined, I will let you go on a patrol. You will ride for weeks, live on beans and salt pork, and may have to fight for your life," Crawford said.

"I will care for the wounded, but I don't think killing the Indians is the answer," Slocum said.

Crawford removed a two-day-old copy of the *Silver City Enterprise* from a basket at the side of his desk and handed it to Slocum. A piece of kindling in the stove popped and sent a shower of sparks. Crawford kicked the stove closed. "Read this. You might change your mind," he said: *Ulzana Escapes from San Carlos Reservation, Strikes Mining Camp and Ranches in Florida Mountains; Dozens Killed.*

"Who is Ulzana?" Slocum asked.

"A Bedonkohe Apache related to Geronimo. He leads a dozen warriors who bitterly hate the Americans for taking their land. They killed two troopers, a scout, and a half dozen miners and ranchers, but the Indians haven't lost a single man. Lieutenant Fountain is going out with C Troop to run him down. They leave in the morning. It will be a short patrol on this side of the border. I suggest you go with Fountain. When you see how rugged it is, you may change your mind about going after Malone," Crawford said.

CHAPTER ELEVEN
Chasing Ulzana

Slocum packed instruments and medicines in a saddle bag along with spare clothing and the Colt revolver. The troop of twenty soldiers and thirty scouts drew up on the parade ground in the half-light of a false dawn. The troopers, splendid in blue uniforms, broad-brimmed hats, boots, and spurs, sat their horses with pride. Zeke had selected a spirited gray mare named Nelly for Slocum, but the doctor was uneasy in the saddle, and in his worn jacket and mended trousers he felt out of place among the snappy cavalrymen.

At the lieutenant's command, the troopers formed a column and, first at a walk, then at a cantor, rode out of the fort while the band played and the men burst into the Irish drinking song.

We can dare or we can do,
United men and brothers too,
Their gallant footsteps to pursue,
And change our country's story.
Our hearts so stout have got us fame,
For soon 'tis known from whence we came,
Where'er we go they dread the name,
Of Garryowen in glory.

The song stirred Tom's heart, and he felt better than he had in weeks. He was finally on a trail that might lead to Billy Malone. The troop set off two abreast. Zeke, with Tom Horn, led the pack mules. When they reached the dirt road leading east, the sun sent out the first orange rays of light from behind distant mountains. It was an easy ride until the scouts picked up a trail of perhaps twenty horses that led across country. The column rode through a desert that was barren of everything except for cactus, dry grass, and scrub plants. Nelly went out of her way to rub against prickly pear, yucca, and Spanish bayonet until Slocum's legs bled from punctures and scratches. At every gully and wash, the mare sat back on her haunches, gathered herself, then launched into a tremendous leap. The first time, Tom almost went sprawling. After that, he held the pommel for dear life. Sometime after noon, Nelly balked, looked back with wild, bulging eyes, then stepped away from a buzzing rattlesnake.

Lieutenant Fountain set a fast pace, and during the late afternoon, the trail led deeper into the Mogollon Mountains. They camped by Mule Springs after dark without fires. Supper was water, dried beef, and rock-hard biscuits. Tom lay down in his bedroll but came awake within a few hours to the sound of the men saddling their horses and grumbling about the lack of hot coffee. The troop got underway without breakfast and plunged deeper into the mountains before dawn, but the trail broke up into different directions.

"Those damn Apaches separated into three groups," Lieutenant Fountain said.

The scouts found the main trail leading up a steep hill along a water course hemmed in by giant boulders. Nelly stepped gingerly from rock to rock or made bone-jerking leaps over downed logs. The stream sides became steeper until the single file column marched in gushing water in the stream bed. As they gained altitude, the desert gave way to a lush green forest studded with giant boulders, steep hillsides, and overhanging cliffs.

When a doe and her fawn broke for cover, the soldiers, expecting an ambush, reached for their weapons. At a waterfall the troops dismounted and led their horses still higher on a faint game trail until they came to a meadow at the end of a long valley.

At noon, a half dozen scouts raced back to the column, and after a palaver with hand signs and pointing, the column went on to the ruins of burned-out cabins clustered around a mine tunneled into a hillside.

"Doctor, do you still think we shouldn't kill the savages?" Lieutenant Fountain asked. The body of a naked man was riddled with bullet holes, and the head was half severed from the neck. The woman's body was covered with bruises; there was a long, deep slash across her belly, and her head was bashed. Brains and blood oozed out on the ground.

"Apaches typically mutilate the men before killing them and take the women and children as slaves. They never take scalps but bash heads so the victim won't recognize them in the afterlife," the lieutenant said.

Slocum gagged and barely held down bile. "Dear God, this is plain murder, not war," he said.

"Help." The feeble cry came from deep within the mine. The sergeant lit a torch and, with two soldiers, went into the dark cave. The man was crouched low behind a rock ledge. His eyes were filled with terror, his body jerked, and he babbled incoherently. Slocum gave the fellow a dose of whisky laced with laudanum. His eyes rolled back, but he wouldn't talk.

The troopers unsaddled their horses and put them out to feed on dry grass and to water at the stream. The men made small cooking fires, and within an hour, beans with pork and molasses were simmering over the coals. Slocum ate his beans and biscuits with the men until his belly was full and then sipped steaming coffee. He was saddle sore and weary to the bone.

"Drag him over here," the lieutenant said. Two soldiers got the survivor to his feet and half dragged him to the officer. Fountain slapped the man's face. When the fellow looked with blank eyes and made no response, the lieutenant slapped him again.

"Let's try whisky and coffee," Slocum said. The poor fellow sunk down on his haunches. His head hung low. Slocum put a cup to his lips. The hot drink spilled down his chin until the fellow gulped convulsively, took in a mouthful, and swallowed. His eyes opened and his muscles loosened.

"Damn you, tell us what happened," Fountain said. For a minute or so, the man's mouth worked but there was no sound. Then, all of a sudden, he found the power of speech.

"They come out of nowhere, fifteen or twenty of them. 'We are good Indians. Give us food and blankets!' they shouted. We thought they were from the reservation," the man said.

"You damn well know there ain't no tame Indians in these parts," Lieutenant Fountain said.

"How was we to know? My partner went to the door with his rifle, but they shot him dead. I ran out the back and got into the mine, but they set the house on fire. I heard the screams when they killed the missus. They got away with the horses and cattle."

"Typical of the damn savages. We will get an early start," Fountain said.

Slocum spread a canvas tarp on the ground, took off his boots, crawled under his saddle blanket, and laid his head on his saddle. Every stone, root, and rock on the mountain dug into his back. He rolled over and used his crushed hat for a pillow. He listened to the rustling of horses and the snoring men. He fell into a half sleep with bad dreams but came wide awake at the hoot of an owl. A coyote yipped. He rested on one elbow and stared at a half-moon floating over the mountaintop. Could it have been an Indian signal? he wondered. The other men were sound asleep, and the guard was humming softly to the horses. Slocum fell back and dreamed that Malone's head was half severed from his body.

Zeke shook him awake in the half-light of a false dawn. His bedroll and hair were covered with frost, and he was stiff with cold. "We are saddlin' up. Here's a cuppa coffee," Zeke said.

Tom, stiff and saddle sore, could hardly walk. Zeke put the saddle on Nelly. Slocum heaved himself up on the horse and rode at the end of the column. The scouts had lost the trail, but they went up another steep defile between two cliffs. The troop followed until they came out on another breathtakingly beautiful valley between tree-studded slopes.

Just before noon, the heavy *boom* of an army carbine and then a scattering of shots came from over the next hill. The troopers formed a line and went up a rise, through an opening in the trees and fired a volley of shots. Slocum urged Nelly to a gallop and came over the hill in time to see the scouts chasing nine or ten yipping Indians who were herding cattle into a canyon. The troopers charged, but the Indians jumped from their horses, disappeared behind boulders, and opened fire. The troopers milled about at the head of the canyon. Two men fell. The rest took cover.

Slocum hung back and swiveled in his saddle when he heard a shot and then a loud, drawn-out scream from a clump of trees off to his right. He spurred his horse toward the sound and saw flames leap from a barn and a tall Indian, with hair down to his shoulders and white streaks painted on his face, emerge from the door of a cabin. The huge Indian clutched the ankles of a screaming boy and dragged the child's head along the ground, then bounded to the corral and swung the child's head against a post. The top of the boy's skull exploded at the impact, and bits of scalp and blood erupted from his head. His scream became a whimper, like the mewing of a cat. The giant Indian swung the boy around his head and flung him into the flames of the burning barn. The mewling cries stopped, and a small arm rose from the flames. The arm sizzled, splattered fat, and burned into a blackened stump.

"Damn you!" Slocum spurred his horse forward and drew the Colt from a saddle bag. He pulled Nelly to a stop a dozen feet from the Indian, aimed, pulled back the hammer of the pistol, and squeezed the trigger. The pistol misfired. He jerked back the hammer and fired at the huge grinning Indian. Nelly danced away as he aimed four more shots. The Indian roared with laughter, leaped on his pony, and galloped into the woods.

The Indians melted away into the mountains, and the cattle scattered into inaccessible canyons. The troopers and scouts gave up the chase and walked their horses back to the cabin. Slocum felt clammy and sick. For a half hour, he had uncontrollable shivering, but he set out his instruments, bandages, and medicines. Slocum cleaned wounds, extracted bullets, and applied carbolized gauze. When the men were settled and comfortable, he cleaned and repacked his instruments. The work kept his mind away from the vision of the boy spinning in a circle and flung, alive, into flames.

They found the rancher's mutilated body behind the cabin. A trooper who went into the brush to relieve himself heard steady sobbing from a ditch. The Indians had stripped and beaten the woman, but she was alive and told how Ulzana's men had driven off the cattle and horses and set fire to the barn. Her husband had fired a few shots, but the Indians riddled him with bullets.

Slocum rested against a sun-warmed boulder near a small fire. He basked in pleasant warmth and thought of Rachel and his young son, but the sight of the maniacal Indian and the boy and his bullet-ridden father would not go away. He groaned at the thought of what the savage Apaches must have done with Billy Malone.

Tom Horn rode up on a handsome stallion accompanied by an Indian scout. "One of my men wishes to speak with you," Horn said.

"Sit down and talk," Tom said.

"This is Chato, a good man. He followed Cochise but decided to live on the reservation and became a scout for General Crook. He speaks some English, but I will interpret for you," Horn said.

Chato, like most of the Apache men, was six feet tall and made of solid bone and muscle. A blue band around his head held his shoulder-length black hair away from his face. A shirt that hung below his knees covered loose trousers that were tucked into buckskin leggings. A striped blanket was wrapped around his waist. Slocum stood and reached out his hand. Chato had an iron-hard grip.

"You are very brave," Chato said.

"Thank you," Slocum replied.

"Not many men would have charged an Apache warrior alone. The woman Das-Te-Sah says you have great healing power." Chato paused and took in every inch of Slocum with his dark, intelligent eyes. "You seek your friend, the Lieutenant Malone."

"Do you know of him?" Slocum asked.

"Let us sit and smoke," Chato said. He removed a long-stemmed pipe from a buckskin bag, filled the bowl with tobacco, lit the pipe with an ember, put it to his lips, drew in smoke, and slowly exhaled. He passed the pipe to Slocum, who took in the acrid tobacco smoke, coughed, and passed the pipe back to Chato, who spoke deliberately and waited for Tom Horn to translate.

"Many years ago, Usan, the Great Spirit, created the Apaches, gave us a home, wild game and plants to eat, healing herbs, and all things needed for a good life. When the white man came, Usan abandoned his people. We suffered hunger, sickness, and many died because of the whites."

Chato paused, took the pipe in both hands, made a cloud of smoke, and again passed the pipe to Slocum. "Sometimes, Usan reminds us of who we are. He comes back to us in the form of an animal, a white buffalo, a white bear. Always, the animal is white so we know it is Usan, our Great Spirit."

There was another long pause. The sun was down behind a peak, and a cold wind whirled through the valley. Tom Horn threw sticks on the fire.

"Your friend, the Lieutenant Malone, was strong, brave, and kind to Apaches. He believed in the Christian God and Jesus. We were high in the mountains, in the clouds. Lieutenant Malone had a fast horse, a very fast horse with sure feet. He was eager to find Geronimo and had ridden up a dry wash and into the mist. I lost sight of him."

Chato paused for several minutes as if he were collecting his thoughts. "There were gunshots. We rode that way down a steep hill to an opening in the trees. We were still high in the mountains in the clouds. While I was looking for Lieutenant Malone, a great white horse came out of the cloud. The white horse had a long mane and a thick, long tail, like silver. He had strong legs, ran fast, and disappeared into the cloud. The white horse was the Great Spirit. He took your friend to the white man's heaven."

Tom stared into the fire long after Horn and Chato left. His hopes had soared but were dashed by the Indian's fanciful story.

After a while, he went to the chuck wagon for beans and coffee. Later, he placed a row of stones on the far side of his fire to reflect heat on his bed roll. The fire kept him warm, but there was frost on his blankets in the morning.

Lieutenant Fountain sent the wounded men and the woman with a squad to the nearest town, Deming. The troopers combed the canyon's dry washes for miles around, but there was no trace of Ulzana or his band. The squad returned from Deming the next day with news that the renegades had cut the telegraph wires. Later, a heliograph on a distant mountain spelled out a message in dots and dashes. Ulzana had attacked another settlement, fifty miles to the west, killed a dozen men, stolen horses, and raided a pack train for supplies.

When it appeared Ulzana was headed for Guadalupe Canyon, Fountain raced to cut off his escape route into Mexico. When the lieutenant saw three renegades herding cattle into the canyon, he sent a squad to head off the Apaches. The men climbed to high ground, but the three Apaches were decoys. Ulzana's main band fired from behind cover and killed five soldiers before the Americans retreated. The Indians were still firing when Tom Slocum reached the victims. The bodies were riddled with bullet holes from the Apache's repeating rifles. This was the end of the campaign. Ulzana slipped through the Sulphur Springs Valley and vanished into Mexico with his dozen warriors and boys. He had outwitted and outrun the entire United States Army.

Nelly behaved and Slocum sat the saddle with confidence when he rode home with the tattered, dispirited soldiers. There were no bugle calls and no singing when the troop rode the final mile into Fort Bowie. Lieutenant Fountain dropped back and came alongside Slocum. "The men appreciate your help," Fountain said.

"Thank you. The whole affair seemed useless," Slocum replied.

"No, not useless. Ulzana lost at least one man. The renegades are forced to use boys as soldiers. That means we are wearing them down. We can always replace our losses, but they

100

have no reserves," Fountain said. Slocum stiffly dismounted at the stables. Zeke led Nelly away to the stable for currying and a well-earned bag of oats.

"Doc, let me see your old pistol. If you are going to charge Apaches single-handed, you need a better weapon," Lieutenant Fountain said.

Slocum dug the Colt out of his saddlebag and handed it to Fountain. "These old cap-and-ball Colts served well in the war but are almost useless now," Fountains said. He put the hammer at half-cock, spun the cylinder, and sighted along the barrel. "No wonder you didn't hit the damn Indian. The cylinder doesn't line up with the barrel. You could kill yourself with this gun."

"A good friend carried it at Shiloh until he lost an arm. I don't have the heart to part with it," Slocum said.

"Do you mind if I take it to our gunsmith?" Fountain asked.

"Go ahead," Slocum replied.

CHAPTER TWELVE

The Reservation

"Sir, I require another hospital steward," Slocum said.

"I can't spare a single man," Lieutenant Crawford said.

"There must be someone," Slocum replied.

"I was about to discharge Sergeant Milligan on account of he has a busted hand and can't shoot. You can have him," Crawford said.

"I can't be choosy. Send him over," Slocum said.

Sergeant Milligan tucked his campaign cap under his arm and touched his hand to his forehead. The salute caused him to grimace with pain. "No need to salute, Milligan, I am a civilian," Slocum said.

Milligan had the three chevrons of a buck sergeant on the sleeve of his dusty jacket. "Me name is Mulligan, Fingal O'Flaherty Mulligan. The recruitin' officer couldn't spell."

Slocum leaned back in his chair and took a closer look at the sergeant. "What is that bit of green ribbon in your cap?"

Milligan, or Mulligan, straightened to his full six feet. "Irish Brigade, sir, Sixty-Ninth New York Volunteers."

"That was a famous outfit in the war. How did you happen to join?" Slocum asked.

"Oh, now, that is a long story. When me pa died, mither took me to Liverpool, and there I sneaked on one of them immigrant ships and hid in the hold for near three days before I got so hungry I was gonna die. A poor old soul gave me bread and gruel. I got off the boat in New York on a cold day without a penny in me pockets."

"How did you get in the army?"

102

"We boyos were walkin' the streets lookin' for work when a fellow said, 'Go through that door for free beer and a sandwich.' Oh, it was grand. A big, fine fellow with a blue suit and brass buttons said, 'Boys, help yourselves.' I finished off a roast beef sandwich and a schooner before you could say 'jack rabbit.' The big fellow said, 'If you want three square meals a day and fine clothes, just sign this here paper.' I put me X on the paper and said my name to the man. That is when he spelled Mulligan, Milligan. 'Well, fellow, you just joined the army,' he said."

"The captain said you can't shoot. What is the matter?" Slocum asked. Mulligan unwrapped a dirty bandage. His right wrist was swollen, dull red, and draining foul green pus. "How did this happen?"

"It is like this, Doc, I went through Bull Run, Malvern Hill, and the wheat field at Gettysburg without a scratch. Last year, I was showing a recruit how to clean his rifle, but the damn fool didn't know it was loaded. He pulled the trigger, and the bullet went through the top of me wrist."

"Move your fingers," Slocum said.

Mulligan flexed and extended his thumb. "It hurts like hell." Slocum pressed the wrist joint. "Oh Jaysus, Doc, that one hurt. The last doctor wanted to cut my arm off."

"In Edinburgh, there were cases like this. An operation might relieve the pain, but you would have a rigid wrist," Slocum said.

"Could I still shoot?" Mulligan asked.

"I think so," Slocum replied.

"Well go on and do the operation."

"Tomorrow morning," Slocum said.

It took almost an entire bottle of ether to put Mulligan asleep before Slocum could scrub the sergeant's arm and hand with lye soap and a solution of carbolic. The incision across the top of the joint opened a pocket of pus where the bullet had hit the radius bone. The infection had destroyed the metacarpal bones and the tip of the ulna. Slocum remembered how Joseph Bell, a surgeon at the Royal Infirmary in Edinburgh, had removed dead, infected bone back to healthy tissue, then jammed the remaining bones together so the healthy bone would become a solid, rigid mass. The joint had no movement but the patient still had a useful hand. Slocum scooped away the dead and infected tissue with a sharp curette until the marrow of the radius and ulna bled freely. He then trimmed cartilage from the metacarpal bones, jammed them into the radius and ulna, and splinted the wrist with heavy bandage and board splints.

At morning rounds, Mulligan had no fever and was as chipper as could be. "Doc, it feels better already," he said.

"You have to wear the splint for three months, but there is no reason why you can't be an assistant hospital steward," Slocum said.

"I will do my best, sir."

"First thing, you must wash your hands with soap and water before you touch a patient, a bandage, or an instrument," Slocum said.

"Ain't nothing wrong with my hands, except I can't move my wrist," Mulligan said.

"Damn it, man, your hands are covered with dirt and the germs that cause sepsis and gangrene," Slocum said.

"I can't see no germs," the sergeant replied.

"If you can't keep clean, I will recommend your discharge from the army," Slocum said.

"Ah, Doc, I don't know nothing else. So help me God, I'll try to be learnin'."

A week later, a soldier broke into sick call, waving a telegram. "Doc, Lieutenant Davis at Fort Apache needs a doctor!" the soldier shouted.

"Well, damn it, what for?" Slocum asked.

"Some men got drunk and beat their wives. Davis says to hurry. One woman is in bad shape," the soldier said.

Zeke and Mulligan packed Slocum's instruments and medicines in a heavy leather saddlebag atop a small mouse-colored mule named Daisy. They set off with Perico, an Apache scout, and Micky Free, a half-Irish, half-Mexican boy who was captured and raised by the Apaches. He spoke English, perfect

Apache, and was fluent in Spanish. "It is over a hundred miles to the reservation. Take us three days, at least," Micky said.

"Chance to see new country," Slocum replied.

They set out that very afternoon under clear skies, but there were soft, white cirrus clouds over the mountains. The scout set a rapid pace on a wide plain east of the Dos Cabeza Mountain Range. Zeke shot an antelope late in the afternoon. That night, they camped in a grove of cottonwoods next to the San Simon River and enjoyed roast antelope loin and beans for supper. Micky Free, a solemn, baby-faced fellow who looked and dressed like an Indian, taught Slocum a few more Apache words. "Tell me about the reservation," Slocum asked.

"In the summer, the tribes camp along a creek with good water in the mountains. It is a fine place: plenty of game, firewood, everything the people need. In the winter, they go down into the valley where it is warmer," Free said.

"It sounds ideal," Slocum said.

"Good, but not good. The women work, but the men gamble and lay around. Sometimes they get drunk, have terrible hangovers, and are mean as grizzly bears with cubs. They fight each other and beat their women. The Apaches don't like to stay in one place. For centuries, they roamed the mountains and deserts, killing animals for food. At first, they were friendly with the whites. Now, they steal cattle and horses for fun and sometimes kill the whites. The Americans say Indians should settle in one place and become farmers," Micky replied.

The next day, the party forded the Gila River. Late on the morning of the fourth day, they reached the winter camp in the low foothills of the White Mountains. The camp was in a pleasant glade near a small stream and was surrounded by giant pine trees. Small brush huts were scattered through the valley and along the stream. Women and children tended cooking fires, and men lazed about smoking and playing games with small bones that looked like dice. There were signs of deer in the hills, and a wild turkey gobbled way off in the distance.

Lieutenant Davis greeted Slocum with a warm handshake in front of his wall tent with boarded-up sides. Davis was a young, square-jawed second lieutenant, not long out of West Point, with a reputation for being honest with the Indians. He was responsible for more than five hundred half-wild Apaches. More than once, he had waded into fights and single-handedly disarmed a drunken warrior.

"Doctor, thank God you are here. I hope you can save this woman," Davis said.

"What is wrong?" Slocum asked.

"Some of the young men got drunk on home-brewed beer and beat their wives. One young lady has a broken arm, a bashed head, and is near death. If she dies, her family will try to kill the husband, and then there will be a big war between the families," Davis said.

At least thirty young Indians with Winchester rifles and long knives jabbered and gestured at Davis. "What is this all about?" Slocum asked.

"They are angry because I sent the woman's husband to jail and said they can't drink beer," Davis replied.

The sick woman lay on a pile of animal skins in a brush hut covered with pieces of canvas. The air was murky with the smoke of burnt turkey feathers. An Indian with a smoldering feather in one hand and a gourd filled with pebbles in the other danced a jig around a bubbling pot over a small fire in the middle of the hut. Slocum batted away the smoke and watched the performance. The gray-haired Indian with a lined face wore a short breechclout. A bear-tooth neckless hung around his neck. For an old fellow, he had strong, sinewy arms and legs. He rattled the gourd in Slocum's face, drew back his lips into a snarl, and hissed like a wildcat.

"Does he bite?" Slocum asked.

"His name is Tudavia, from the Warm Springs Tribe. He heals wounds that would defy most doctors, but this lady is getting worse," Davis said. She was no more than eighteen, slender, with even features and raven-black hair. She could be beautiful. Slocum wondered how any man could beat his wife. The woman moaned, opened her eyes for a moment, and turned away.

"Can you help her?" Davis asked.

"She probably has a concussion and is septic from the wounds." Slocum backed out of the hut. "Any way I can talk with Tudavia?" he asked.

"Micky Free can interpret," Davis said.

"Tell him I want to learn how he heals wounds," Slocum said.

Micky and old Tudavia palavered for a half hour. "He says he cannot tell his secrets to a white man, but he will show you a wound he healed in a man that would be dead under a white man's treatment," Micky said.

Tudavia motioned to a muscular, young Indian. Tudavia pounded on the man's chest. "See, a bullet went through his heart, but he lived." Sure enough, there was an old scar from a bullet wound on the left chest, and the bullet was lodged between two ribs on the man's back. The bullet had, indeed, gone through the man's left chest, and it appeared to be a miraculous cure. Slocum remembered a case from medical school in Chicago. He put his ear to the man's chest and heard the heart's *thump, thump* on the right side. The heart and all the organs were on the wrong side. It was a case of situs inversus. The bullet had passed through the lung but missed the heart.

"I have greater medicine," Slocum said. "Without looking, I can tell the right testicle of this man hangs lower than the left. The left testicle of every man here, except this man, is lower," Slocum cried. Every man, including Lieutenant Davis, grabbed his crotch.

"See, every one of you is the same, except for this man. His heart is on the right side. The bullet never hit the heart," Slocum said. While the onlookers shuffled and muttered, Davis offered a cigarette to the medicine man. Slocum quickly took a Lucifer from his shirt pocket, scratched it on the seat of his tough canvas pants, and lit Tudavia's cigarette with great ceremony. The old medicine man took the blackened matchstick and recoiled as if he had been shot.

"The white doctor lit the piece of wood by blowing flames from the little hole in his back. He has powerful medicine. I

107

teach him Apache medicine if he teaches me to make fire from the little hole in my back," Tudavia said.

"Tell Tudavia that only white men have this power, but I will show him medicine that is stronger than whisky or beer," Slocum said.

"He says that is good," Micky said.

"Mulligan, the ether and a bit of gauze," Slocum said.

The doctor poured an ounce of ether on the gauze and held it to the Indian's face. "Tell him to breathe deep," Slocum said.

The old boy took deep breaths and commenced to giggle, roared with laughter, then slumped to the ground, sound asleep. "Enough," Slocum said.

Tudavia awoke with a silly grin. "Medicine work faster than whisky," he said.

"Mulligan, bring the bull's-eye lantern and my instruments," Slocum said.

"Do you need anything else, sir?" he asked.

"Hold the light." The doctor knelt by the woman. She was beyond pain, and blood from a jagged scalp wound clotted in her hair. Her left eye was swollen shut from a great bruise on her cheek, but the worst was a jagged wound through torn muscle down to her left shoulder joint that drained thick green pus. Her collarbone was broken. "Tell Tudavia to sing a healing song while I work on the wounds," Slocum said.

There was no need for anesthesia. Slocum swabbed the wounds with gauze soaked in carbolic. Surprisingly, beneath Tudavia's poultice, the scalp wound was clean, but dirt and wood splinters were ground into the depths of the shoulder wound. "He beat her with a chunk of firewood," said Davis.

Slocum removed splinters, bits of cloth, and dirt, then cut away dead necrotic muscle. "Mulligan, more carbolic," he said.

"Doc, there ain't no more. The bottle was only half full," Mulligan said.

"Oh, damn," Slocum said. Old Tudavia had kept up a steady monotonous drone while doing a jig about the fire. "Have Micky ask how he makes his poultice."

Old Tudavia grinned and held out two hands and pointed to the kettle simmering over the fire. "He boils two handfuls of the root of snakeroot in fresh spring water in a copper kettle until half the water is gone."

"It is worth trying," Slocum said. He plucked a soft mass of roots and twigs from the bubbly green liquid with forceps. When the mess cooled, he packed the shoulder wound and splinted the arm to the woman's chest. Tudavia stopped singing, and in a moment, the young woman opened her eyes with the startled expression of a fawn. Tudavia spoke a few words, and she went back to sleep.

"Amazing. Must be a sort of hypnosis," Slocum exclaimed.

"I shot a young wild turkey for dinner. Time to eat," Davis said.

At first light in the morning, Slocum pushed aside the canvas door and stepped inside the woman's hut. Old Tudavia was chanting in a soft voice. At Slocum's touch, the young woman opened her eyes. She instantly sat upright and stared at Slocum like he was a stranger from the moon. Her skin was cool and dry. She had no fever.

At breakfast with Davis, Slocum sopped up bacon grease with a corn pone. "That woman should be dead by now. It is a damn miracle she is alive," he said.

"I am not surprised. Old Tudavia has healing powers, and sometimes he predicts the future. Ask him about your friend after we pass out the weekly rations," Davis said.

The wagons carrying the Indian' weekly rations were drawn up near the river. Government-appointed civilian agents set out their weights and measures. A crowd of half-naked, dirty, semi-starved children and sullen, older Indian women with pots and deerskin bags for the weekly issue of beef and flour edged closer to agents. The flour, beans, coffee, and sugar were supposed to last them for a week. Civilians guarding the agents, armed with Winchesters, bandoliers of cartridges, and revolvers, stood back in the brush, stolidly watching the proceedings.

The agents were supposed to issue a pound of flour for every man, woman, and child, but they fiddled the weights and passed out short rations that would not last the week. At midmorning, yipping cowboys herded twenty skinny cows from a ranch a few miles away. The cattle stopped in the river and drank water until their flanks were swollen. When the cattle were weighed, they were half water. "The bastards cheat," Slocum exclaimed.

Davis shook his head. "The army has no control over the civilian agents. They sell supplies meant for the Indians to white miners and ranchers. The politicians support them," he replied. Men shot the cows in the head and set to work butchering the skin-and-bone animals. Old women stood by to grab bits and morsels of gut, liver, and kidney to cook up with roots, bones, and berries in a stew.

Slocum and Micky Free found Tudavia smoking his pipe by a small fire at the outskirts of the camp. Slocum offered the old man a pouch of tobacco. "My best friend is a brave, good man. He joined the army not to kill Indians but to help. Can you tell if he is dead or alive?" Slocum asked.

"I will require one day and one night." Tudavia held up two fingers. "Two Spanish silver pesos would help," he said.

Slocum handed over two silver dollars. Tudavia grunted, "Not enough. Need more for the women."

"Why women?" Slocum asked.

"The women will heat stones for his sweat lodge," Free said.

Slocum held out a third silver dollar. "Enough?" he asked. Tudavia grunted again. During the afternoon, three old women heated rocks the size of a man's head until they were red hot, then rolled the rocks into Tudavia's low hut. The old man poured water from gourds onto the rocks until the hut was filled with hot steam. Tudavia chanted all afternoon and night.

"You won't see him again until tomorrow," Davis said.

"I hope it is worth three dollars," Slocum replied.

"After dinner, there will be a dance to keep up the fighting spirit of the young men. It is worth watching," Davis said.

The huge bonfire in the middle of a clearing sent sparks high into the dark sky. Davis, Slocum, and Mulligan leaned against trees well back from the dance ring. Five men at the edge of the clearing beat rawhide stretched over drums while chanting a high-pitched song that varied in rhythm. At intervals, the music stopped and a drummer called out a name. Mangus, son of the great chief Mangus Colorado—naked except for a breechclout but painted with red and white stripes—jumped into a ring and walked in a circle around the fire. More men followed until thirty or more fighters, wildly stooping almost to the ground on bent knees, whooped, jumped, and danced. Each man carried a rifle or a bow with a quiver of arrows. The dancers formed a line and advanced, shaking and brandishing their rifles and bows. When the drummers abruptly stopped, the men fired their rifles or sent steel-tipped arrows into the air. Soon, small boys joined the line of dancers and, with arms swinging and knees pumping, kept up with the men. Slocum thought back to his own boyhood when he and his fellows went into the woods and staged mock wars. The party was still in full force when Slocum gave up and went to bed sometime after midnight.

He went to Tudavia's wickiup shortly after first light. The old man chanted in a low voice until the noonday sun reached its peak. Tudavia crawled from the hut, blinked his eyes against the bright sun but looked as chipper and fresh as a boy on his first date. "Tobacco," he said. Slocum gave him a plug twisted into a cigar and scratched a match across the seat of his pants. Tudavia grunted, opened his eyes wide, and, without comment, took several puffs on the crude cigar and spit.

"Tell me about my friend," Slocum said.

Tudavia smoked the cigar down to a small stub before replying. "I am only an Indian and don't know the ways of white men. I spoke with the spirits, but the picture is cloudy."

"Did you gain knowledge about my friend?" Slocum asked.

"Your friend is alive but in danger. He went south on a great white horse."

Slocum reeled back as if he had been shot. "How could this old man tell a story so similar to Chato's?"

Lieutenant Davis clasped Slocum's shoulder. "He has made many astounding predictions. Sometimes I believe these old men have supernatural powers," he said.

Slocum was further mystified when the woman's wound rapidly healed after five days of repeated applications of the snake-root poultice. Even stranger was her rapid recovery from the concussion. On his last visit, she prepared a pot of stew over an open fire for three scrawny kids.

"She looks fine. Time for me to leave," Slocum said.

"Thanks for your help," Davis said.

Geronimo and Naiche after the surrender at Fort Bowie

Geronimo with a single-shot Springfield rifle. This was a posed photo after he was disarmed.

Chato, a warrior who became a trusted scout

Apache scouts, dressed for action and well-armed

Captain Gatewood with spiked shako and dress uniform

Captain Emmett Crawford, who commanded the scouts and was killed in action

Mules with packs in typical hilly terrain

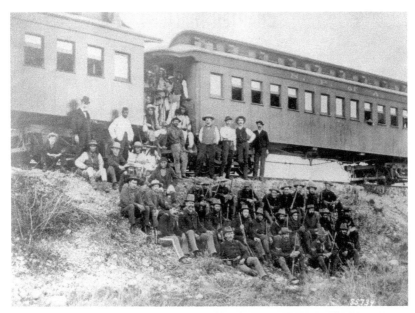

Train at siding loading Apaches for trip east to prison in Florida

Wickiups, easily constructed with branches and grass and covered with animal skins, were suitable for the Apache's nomadic life. In more permanent camps, they used tepees more typical of the Plains Indians.

119

CHAPTER THIRTEEN
Ambush

Lieutenant Crawford threw the *Tombstone Epitaph* on the floor of the officer's mess. "Damn, the war department and Grover Cleveland, the first damn Democrat to be elected president since the war blames Crook for Ulzana's murderous rampage. The governor of Arizona is calling out the state militia," Crawford exclaimed.

"Damn fools don't understand," another officer muttered.

To make matters worse, that afternoon a courier galloped into the post on a hard-ridden horse. "Breakout at San Carlos! Apaches on the warpath and headin' to Mexico!" he shouted. Officers and men ran from their quarters, strapping on holsters and swords.

"They will join Geronimo. I will get him, dead or alive," Crawford said.

"Crook has stationed troops at every water hole along the border to capture any Indian who tries to get into Mexico. It will take a major operation to find Geronimo and bring his band to the reservations," Lieutenant Fountain said.

Rumors about the impending expedition into Mexico flew about the fort. The new recruits wildly overestimated the numbers and power of the Apache and were deathly afraid. The line for morning sick call extended out the door of the hospital and around to the side of the building. At first, Slocum thought there was an epidemic of contagious disease, but none of the men were acutely ill.

The young buck private clutched the side of his chest and barked out a deep cough. "Doc, I got this terrible cough and my side hurts like hell. I can't sleep," the soldier said. Slocum looked into his mouth, made him gag to take a look at his throat and tonsils, then listened to both lungs, pounded on the boy's chest, and listened to the sounds of air moving back and forth in the bronchial tubes. The lungs and throat were perfectly normal.

"Ain't nothing wrong with you. The cough could be from breathing dust," Slocum said.

"Oh, but Doctor, I hurt something terrible. I can't ride a horse in my condition."

Slocum gave the man a bottle of cherry-flavored water. "Take this and come back if you don't get better," he said.

The next man stepped before the desk. "It's my back. Ever since I fell off my horse, I can't straighten up. Terrible pain, nothing helps," he said. Slocum examined the man's back, checked for muscle spasm, weakness of the legs, and the reflexes. When he tapped the boy's knees, the leg kicked out. It was all perfectly normal. All that morning, Slocum listened to a litany of upset stomachs, backaches, headaches, foot spasms, coughs, and strange symptoms that weren't in medical books. Every man wanted a paper that said they couldn't ride and should go on light duty.

On the third morning, in desperation, Slocum gave each man an ounce of castor oil mixed with cascara sagrada, a powerful laxative. Most men made it to the latrines; others, unable to hold it in, dropped their britches out in the field and let go with liquid diarrhea. The epidemic of malingering stopped.

General Crook assigned Captain Crawford to lead the expedition into Mexico to find Geronimo and his band. Lieutenant Marion Maus, a West Point man, was second in command. Lieutenant Fountain led B company, and Tom Horn was chief of the Indian scouts. Pete, with Zeke, his new assistant, was in charge of the mule train. The general invited all the officers and Dr. Slocum, now an official surgeon, to dinner. After the meal, he issued orders. "March into Mexico, track the renegades, kill the men, and bring the women and children back to the reservation. Stay in Mexico six months if necessary," Crook said.

Lieutenant Fountain came to the hospital on the morning after Slocum had treated the malingerers to castor oil. "Things

121

are going to get hot on this expedition. You may have to defend yourself," the lieutenant said.

"There will be plenty of soldiers around; I am not worried," Slocum replied.

"The gunsmith bored out the cylinder of your pistol to take thirty-two/twenty brass cartridges and tightened up the barrel. It shoots straight. Watch this," Fountain said. He tossed a tin can toward an empty field and, with the other hand, fired Slocum's pistol from the hip. The can spun in the air from the bullet's impact and hit the ground. Fountain fired again. The can shot two feet in the air, landed, and bounced. Fountain emptied the gun. There were five bullet holes in the can.

"My God, that is great shooting; you didn't even aim," Slocum said.

Fountain slid fresh brass cartridges into the cylinder and passed the gun to Slocum. "Shoot by instinct. Don't aim, keep your eyes on the target, and simply point the gun and ignore the sights. Concentrate on the target. Your hand and the gun will point to the target," Fountain said. Slocum missed the first five shots, but by the end of the afternoon, he punched holes in the can at least half the time.

The thirty soldiers and three companies of Apache scouts left the fort before dawn. Balky mules held up the line until Pete kicked his lead mule, an old mare with a bell around her neck. She got underway, the bell tinkled in time with her gate, and, after a while, the mules followed.

Tom, on Nelly, and Sergeant Mulligan leading Daisy carrying medical supplies, jogged along in the middle of the line of two-abreast troopers. Slocum had learned Nelly's whims and rode with more confidence. He carried the Colt revolver in a holster.

The morning was clear and cold, but the well-beaten trail that led southeast on the plain that skirted the spiky peaks of the Chiricahua Mountains was easy to follow. Slocum turned in his saddle to marvel at a huge saguaro cactus. "They look like men," he said.

"Well, sir, according to an Apache legend, a mither lost her child in the desert. The little fellow took root and growed up to be a cactus," Mulligan said.

The trail turned south and threaded through boulders the size of railroad engines and tangles of dense, thorny brush that tore at the horses and men. Slocum jogged alongside Lieutenant Fountain to pass the time. Fountain swept his arm around the horizon.

"This whole area is the ancestral ground of the Chiricahua band of Apaches. Cochise fought the Mexicans, white settlers, and the army for years but finally gave up after the army promised him this land for a reservation." Fountain pointed to the west. "Over that mountain is Tombstone. There was nothin' there but a few ranchers until an ex-army man found a vein of silver right on the surface. A whole swarm of miners drove the Apaches away. It was a damn shame," Fountain said.

"There could be a hundred Apaches up that ravine, in those rock formations. They travel at night and, during the day, hide in arroyos near water holes back in the hills. They never make a stand but shoot from behind cover and then scatter when we approach," Fountain said.

The column moved at a slow pace, while the cowboys settled the mule train and spare horses. Tom Horn, with the Apache scouts, ranged ahead searching for tracks but found no signs of Geronimo's band.

At dawn on the third day, the Guadalupe Mountains rose out of a blue haze to the south. Slocum finished his coffee and climbed a butte with Captain Crawford for a clearer view of the line of march that lay ahead. Crawford searched the Guadalupe Pass with his field glasses. "Doc, focus on the box canyon to the right," he said.

Slocum adjusted the field glasses and caught a glimpse of Indians furiously herding cattle into the deep canyon. "By damn, we can get their cattle and starve the bastards," Crawford said.

Crawford sent Lieutenant Fountain with a squad of soldiers and scouts to capture the cattle. The men looked forward to fresh beef for dinner. The column mounted up and hurried forward. Slocum caught his horse and, with Mulligan, was near the rear of the troop. When furious gunfire broke out, the bugler sounded the charge. The men whooped and urged their mounts

to a gallop. The advance squad was well into the blind canyon
when the main body reached a grove of cottonwood and mesquite trees between two steep cliffs strewn with tumbled boulders. The Apaches, hidden among the rocks, raked the soldiers
with rapid-firing Winchesters. The soldiers fired at puffs of gun
smoke in the rocks but with no effect. A trooper threw up his
hands and slid off his saddle; more fell under the withering firs.

"Mulligan, men are wounded. Let's go!" cried Slocum.

The downed men were on the ground. The troopers madly
returned fire from horseback. The sound of gunfire and horse
hooves drowned out Crawford's cry, "Dismount, take cover!"

War whoops and gunfire erupted from deep within the
canyon. The Indians drove a herd of wild-eyed, ferocious, long-
horned cattle into the midst of the troopers. A stallion reared up.
With his guts dragging in the dirt, the soldier's boot was caught
in the stirrup, and another wild-eyed steer gored his chest.

Slocum leaped off Nelly. "Mulligan, take the supplies behind
the trees!" he shouted. Slocum dragged a gun-shot soldier to
shelter. Another man staggered out of the melee and dropped at
Slocum's side. "Mulligan, bandages and a tourniquet!"

Slocum packed gauze and twisted tourniquets to stop the
torrents of blood from gaping gunshot wounds. "They are getting away! Stop them!" Captain Crawford shouted.

Women in long dresses carrying bundles and papoose baskets, with children running at their sides, climbed a narrow
zigzag path leading up the near-vertical canyon side. One by
one, they reached the ridgeline and disappeared. Another round
of furious rifle fire sent the soldiers scurrying to cover. They
regrouped and fired volleys into the Apaches' hiding places.
There was a lot of noise, but none of the soldiers' bullets found
a mark. When the firing died down, one by one the warriors
sneaked from boulder to boulder. When they reached more open
ground, they bounded like mountain goats up the steep cliff.
The Apaches paused just below the ridgeline, behind boulders
and scrub trees, and fired into the soldiers. When the troopers
were about halfway up the cliff, the Indians rolled boulders and
stones down the trail. Stones the size of a man's head struck the

troopers, who tumbled back down the trail. In a moment, the Indians disappeared.

Slocum knelt by a man and desperately poked a finger into a bullet wound in the throat. The stream of gushing blood from the carotid artery slowed to a trickle and stopped. He was too late; the man was dead.

At the sound of a sliding rock, Slocum glanced away from his work. He looked square into the black, hostile eyes of a savage with a drawn bow standing in a shadow between two giant boulders less than twenty feet away. The warrior, in a long breechclout, leggings, and moccasins, aimed a vicious, iron-tipped arrow directly at Slocum's chest. The doctor reached for his pistol but recognized the long scar and cross-hatched suture marks across Yanuza's bare chest and dropped his hand away from the gun. He locked eyes with Yanuza for a long minute. The boy lowered his bow and, like a shadow, disappeared among the rocks.

Slocum wiped his face with the back of his hand and set to work. During the rest of the day, he cleaned and sutured wounds, set broken bones, and gave morphine to the hopelessly wounded to ease their departure from the living.

When at last he and Mulligan had done their best, he sprawled on the ground in the shadow of a great cottonwood tree. A phrase of schoolboy Latin leaped into his thoughts. *Media vita in morte sumus* [In the midst of life, we are in death]. The fight was over, but as the men caught their mounts and regrouped, a shot rang out from midway up the cliff. A puff of smoke marked the location of the sniper. The men took cover, and two more bullets clipped a tree that hid soldiers. The men poured fire into the sniper's hiding place, and when there were no return shots, the men moved up the cliff, running from one bit of cover to the next.

"It is a woman. She is wounded," a trooper called down. Slocum filled his pockets with bandages and a bottle of carbolic. He was breathing heavily and his muscles burned by the time he reached the pile of rocks in front of a small cave. The young Apache woman, lying in a pool of blood, covered a month-old baby with her body and snarled at the men like a cornered wild-cat. Two soldiers held her while Slocum examined the wound. A heavy bullet had shattered her kneecap, passed through the joint, and exited through a gaping wound at the back of her leg. The scouts rigged a stretcher and carried the woman and her baby to the makeshift aid station. Her leg, below the wound, was already showing signs of gangrene and would have to be removed to save the woman's life. Slocum put out the long amputation knife, bone saw, forceps, needles, and sutures on clean towels. Taklishim, a sergeant of scouts, spoke enough English to interpret for the doctor.

"Explain to her that I will give her sleep medicine, so she will feel no pain," Slocum said.

The woman twisted and spit, then erupted into angry screams. "She says cut off the leg, it is useless," Taklishim said.

She twisted away when Slocum attempted to give her morphine and refused to breathe the ether. She relaxed, took deep breaths, and lay quite still while Mulligan held her leg and Slocum made the skin incision above the knee. He cut through the skin, pulled back the flaps, and, with one quick slash, cut through the thick quadriceps muscle to the bone, then ligated the veins and arteries. The woman winced only once, when he sawed through the femur two inches above the knee joint. After one last swab of the wound with carbolic, he sutured the skin flaps and bandaged the wound. The ordeal lasted ten minutes.

Sergeant Taklishim put the baby in her arms. She struggled to sit upright, and the baby immediately suckled at her breast.

Slocum had coffee and beans by a small bonfire with Lieutenant Fountain, Pete, and Zeke. "That just goes to show, those people are half wild animals. Why, I seen a trapped wolf chew off his own leg that was caught in a trap. That woman didn't show no more pain than that damn wolf," Pete said.

"That was only a rear guard; women, children, and a half dozen warriors. They got away without a single fatality. They will run until Geronimo reaches a safe camp," Fountain said. The wounded men cried for water and morphine during the long night hours. Slocum adjusted splints, redressed wounds, and closed the eyes of two more men who died in the night. The woman stared at him with angry eyes every time he checked her wound. In the morning, the captain sent the most seriously wounded by travois back to Fort Bowie, and the troop rested for the ride into Mexico. The scouts placed the woman, with the baby in her arms, on a mule. She made no complaint and rode all day.

The detachment set off through arroyos with sharp rocks and sandy dry washes. There were few water holes, and brackish water made the men sick. The scouts picked up the trail of the fleeing renegades that led higher in the mountains. "They are running like hell. We ain't likely to catch them," said Tom Horn.

The trail led to three dead herders and charred bones from twenty sheep that the Apaches had roasted over a great bonfire. After feasting all night, the Indians burned another ranch and killed the rancher and his wife, then fled into the mountains with enough horses and mules to mount the entire band.

The Indians again ambushed the troop just south of the Mexican border, east of the San Louis Mountains. They killed four more soldiers but, like wisps of smoke, disappeared into the mountains. Thus far, the American force had not killed a single Apache.

On the second day following this encounter, the scouts trailed the band to the San Janos River, a dry streambed that ran through a deep canyon. Mulligan pointed to black dots in the sky a mile or so ahead. "Them turkey vultures are circling over dead meat, or I'll eat me hat," he said.

Slocum shaded his eyes, and yes, a flock of vultures made lazy circles in the clear sky. Slocum rode ahead to Lieutenant Crawford. "Sir, those vultures are circling up ahead and off to our left. Might be worth investigating," Slocum said.

"Probably more dead sheep or cattle, but I'll send a squad to investigate," Crawford said.

"There may be wounded," Slocum said. He joined Tom Horn with ten scouts and picked his way through dense brush into a shallow valley. The vultures were on the ground a quarter mile ahead; the sickening odor of death hovered over the valley. The scouts set up a terrible wail—and then shouts of anger—when they reached the bloated bodies with pecked-out eyes leaving ghastly empty sockets. Most of the bodies had been scalped. Not only vultures, but the coyotes and other animals had left only rib cages of some of the bodies that were once Apache women and children. Entire families had fallen together in the dry creek bed. The women and children lay on their backs in pools of blood. Up a slight hill, behind a tree, lay a dead, elderly Apache man surrounded by empty brass cartridges.

"Damn Mexicans did this. They caught the women and children away from the main band. The Mexican government pays a hundred pesos for an Apache scalp," Tom Horn said.

"But some of the Apaches are good people. Do they kill all of them?" Slocum asked.

"Makes no difference. They kill our government scouts whenever they have the chance," Horn said. A great anguished cry went up from the scouts. "Corporal Ta-Say recognized his aunt and cousin," Horn said.

Half the scouts raced off toward Janos, the nearest Mexican town, to seek vengeance. Those who remained followed a trail of cooking utensils, blankets, and clothing left by the fleeing Apaches to a series of pits dug into the dry creek bed. From the amount of blood and empty brass rifle cartridges, Geronimo and his band must have returned to protect the women and children; A dozen or more dead Mexicans were heaped up beyond the creek. The scouts galloped back from the Mexican village with whoops and hollers. They had killed two Mexican soldiers and looted a cantina. That night, there was an uproar when the scouts got drunk on the fiery Mexican whisky.

The Apaches broke up into small groups and fled up steep paths and streambeds to the high plateau of the Sierra Madre Mountains. Crawford sent Tom Horn, the best trackers, and forty hand-picked scouts, with extra rations and plenty of ammunition, to find the main band. The rest of the column struggled through deep canyons into the wildest part of the Sierra Madre Mountains, with peaks reaching to nine thousand feet. Slocum treated men with concussions, snake bites, broken bones, and deep lacerations resulting from falls onto sharp rocks. Nelly was sure-footed and kept to the narrow paths that led over summits. One day followed another, with no sign of Geronimo or Billy Malone.

The scouts had another skirmish with Mexican soldiers, but the Mexicans were poor shots, and the scouts returned to the main force with no injuries. The next day, Slocum and Mulligan were plodding along a narrow path when the pack mules brayed, howled, and went berserk after running into a black bear and her cubs. "Them mules are plumb scared of bears," Mulligan said. In the melee, three mules rolled over the precipice and crashed a thousand feet below into a deep ravine, leaving broken saddlebags, flour, and dried beef scattered over the rocks. The troop did without coffee and went on half rations until the scouts slaughtered a mule. Slocum was hungry enough to try anything. Mule meat, simmered with beans and hot chilies, was not bad.

Near the end of December, in a driving rain, Crawford made camp on a plateau near a good spring and grass for the animals. A break came when Lieutenant Fountain visited a ranch to buy cattle and heard the news that Geronimo was camped forty miles away, beyond the Aros River. On the trail to the Apache camp over the Espinazo del Diablo [Devil's Backbone], the scouts discovered carcasses of butchered cattle and then a trail of buckskin-shod mules, typical of Geronimo.

The next day, Tom Horn sniffed the air. "I smell Indians," he said. The scout set out with four of his best men, and that night he spotted campfires on a plateau across a wide valley. He and his men sneaked closer to people from both Naiche's and Geronimo's bands. They had joined forces and had plenty of horses and cattle. Horn hurried back and reported to Crawford.

"We will attack at dawn, kill or capture the lot, and end this damn war," Crawford said. Every man carried a hundred rounds of ammunition, and the men wore soft moccasins to avoid noise. Tom Horn knew the land, and Crawford put him in charge of the attack. Slocum carried a pack filled with basic instruments and supplies and hiked all night. Mulligan stayed behind with the pack mule.

An hour before dawn, and less than a mile from the Apache's camp, Horn divided the force into four groups, with Crawford to the north and Maus to the south. Fountain was to start the fight on the right side, nearest the river, and drive the Indians into Crawford's squad.

Slocum set up an aid station in a sheltered spot and settled down to wait for full daylight. As an afterthought, he checked to see if his Colt was fully loaded. At first light, women emerged from the wickiups to stir up the morning fires. No men were in sight. The Americans held their fire. All was well until a dog followed a woman, stretched, scratched, and then stared straight at the still-invisible line of soldiers and yipped once. Every dog set up terrific barking that brought the Apache warriors and more women and children out of their wickiups.

The eager scouts commenced firing at the renegades. An old man ran through the camp and jumped on a boulder. A cry went up from the scouts. "Geronimo! Geronimo!"

Every scout and every soldier fired, but Geronimo didn't flinch. "Run! Run, to the river!" he shouted. The Indians ran like rabbits, zigging and zagging until they splashed across the river to disappear in dense brush. Geronimo leaped from his perch and followed his people. He did indeed lead a charmed life. There must have been a hundred rifles aimed at him, but he was not hit, not even once.

The Americans killed three women and as many children until Horn swore at the scouts to stop shooting. The scouts ran down and captured more women; one turned out to be a wife of Geronimo. Her child was his son. One lame old man couldn't keep up with the fleeing Apaches but made his way across the river, where he quit running and gave himself up. It was Nana, a famous chief who was near ninety years old and limped from an old leg wound.

"I am no longer fit for war. I will run no more and will fight no more," the old chief said. Nana swung his rifle over his head and slammed it down on a rock. The stock broke away, and he bent the barrel. "Here, take my weapon," he said.

The Indians abandoned their food, cooking utensils, blankets, and even guns and ammunition. The American soldiers were glassy-eyed with fatigue, and some had bloody feet after the forced night march, but Crawford ordered them to pursue the enemy.

"Captain, these men can't go another mile. They need food and rest," Slocum said.

Crawford snapped his jaws like a wolf. "I didn't ask your opinion. I am in command here," he said.

"Sir, I am completely out of ether and haven't enough bandages and antiseptic for more casualties. You are in command, but I am responsible for the health of these men," Slocum said.

The rest of the troop and the pack train straggled in, dismounted, and slumped to the ground. Most were sound asleep and snoring within minutes. Meantime, the scouts divided up the loot that the Apaches had stolen from the Mexicans. What they didn't want went into a huge bonfire. Before long, they roasted a captured pony over the fire for a feast. Captain Crawford gave up pursuing the enemy when tumbling gray clouds brought driving sleet and rain. The soldiers and scouts finished off the pony, beans, and chilies the Apaches left behind. With his belly full, Tom Slocum rigged a canvas shelter and slept soundly until daylight. It was pouring rain, and there was a ten-inch tarantula beneath his bedroll.

Crawford was as hollow-eyed and gaunt as any of the men. Tom Horn, after talking with old Nana, conferred with the officers. "Nana and the women say Geronimo is tired of fighting. They have nothing left and want to talk with the captain. They will wait for you on the ridge behind the white rocks," he said.

Crawford let the men rest and sent to Nacori, the nearest Mexican town, for supplies. He separated twenty-five scouts and a squad of soldiers to take the prisoners and wounded back to Fort Bowie. Slocum was astonished to see his patient, the young woman with an amputated leg, hopping about the camp on crutches. She could climb on a mule with no difficulty.

CHAPTER FOURTEEN
The White Horse

The scouts found the renegade camp less than five miles away, over two ridges and through another boulder-strewn canyon. One of Geronimo's women came out of the camp and spoke with Horn. "Geronimo and the people are tired of running. He will talk with the Tall Captain," she said.

Tom Horn left the main body of scouts a few hundred yards from Geronimo and Naiche's people He reported to Captain Crawford. "Geronimo trusts you and will talk," Horn said.

When the troop topped the last ridge, the white rocks were in sight less than a quarter mile away. Crawford led the men to a level, wooded area beneath a low, brush-covered hill that rose to the whitish boulders off to the right. Just as the men dismounted, rifle fire erupted. Three scouts fell before the intense hail of bullets.

"Damn, Geronimo sucked us into another ambush," Mulligan said.

Slocum picked up the last of his medical supplies and dashed to the aid of the wounded Apache scouts. The scouts returned fire with their Springfield carbines and shouted, "Mexicans! Mexicans!"

The hillside swarmed with men wearing wide sombreros arrayed in front of a squadron of mounted dragoons partly hidden by trees and brush. "Them Tarahumara Injuns are tough bastards and they hate the Apaches," Mulligan said.

"Apaches got no cojones. We take your scalps and women!" the Mexicans yelled. The scouts loaded their single-shot carbines, aimed, and fired with deadly accuracy, but there were hundreds of Mexicans hidden in the brush and behind rocks.

"Geronimo, help!" the scouts shouted. The Apaches, with their rapid-firing Winchesters, poured bullets into the Mexicans, who went down like scythed corn. The survivors turned tail and ran. Geronimo's men came out of hiding from among the rocks to chase the fleeing Mexicans.

"Tell them to stop firing!" Crawford shouted.

Tom Horn ran to the hillside, waving a white handkerchief. *"No tiré, no tiré! Estamos Norte Americanos* [Don't shoot! Don't shoot! We are North Americans]!" he shouted. The force of the bullet spun Horn halfway around; he went down on one knee but arose and again shouted, *"Estamos Norte Americanos!"*

Captain Crawford, also with a white flag, leaped on a small boulder. "Don't shoot! Stop the firing!" he shouted. The scouts stopped shooting, and for a moment the Mexicans held their ground. A Mexican dragoon hidden in the trees fired a single shot that struck Crawford's head. The Tall Captain fell backward, his arms waving in the air. He dropped onto the dirt and rocks beside the boulder. Slocum ran to his side. Crawford was breathing, but the bullet had smashed his forehead. He was unconscious, and the pupil of his left eye was widely dilated. Pink brain tissue and bits of skull dribbled down over the captain's face, and blood pooled in the sand.

"Mulligan, bring up the supplies!" Slocum shouted.

The sergeant gathered bandages and instruments and ran forward to the line of battle. "I am afraid he is a goner," Slocum said. He gently wiped away dirt and removed bits of skull, then wrapped the captain's bleeding head with rolls of bandage.

The Apache scouts, furious at the murder of Crawford, dashed after the Mexicans, firing as they ran. When they ran out of ammunition, they slashed the Mexicans with long knives. Geronimo's band, who had watched the fight from behind the white rocks, erupted in fury and poured more fire from their Winchester repeaters into the Mexican troops. The stunned Mexicans huddled behind rocks and trees but were no match for the howling Apaches.

"The bastards!" Mulligan roared. The Irish sergeant tore off his splint, picked up a rifle from a fallen soldier, and pumped

133

bullets into the Mexicans. Every bullet hit its mark. The slaughter continued for half an hour. Slocum huddled behind a bullet-pocked boulder and held pressure on Crawford's wound to stem the bleeding until four soldiers carried the captain to safety.

There was no let-up in the firing until Tom Horn, again waving a white handkerchief, walked into the melee. "*No tiré!* Cease fire!" he shouted.

The scouts and Geronimo's men continued shooting until a Mexican captain walked toward the American line with a white flag. "We thought you were all Apaches," he said. Horn, Maus, and Fountain called away the furious scouts, but Geronimo's men, who were all for killing every Mexican, continued firing. Horn had a flesh wound in his upper arm, and there were three wounded scouts. Nearly fifty Mexicans were dead, and more were wounded.

"Can your doctor help our men?" the Mexican captain asked. Slocum used the last of the morphine and bandages on the Mexican wounded and, at the far end of the battlefield, he came upon a sergeant sitting half upright against a downed tree. As Slocum approached, the Mexican drew a fully cocked revolver and aimed at Slocum.

"*Hijo de puta* [son of a whore]," he said. The doctor kicked the big Colt out of the man's hand.

"I am a doctor," Slocum said.

The man gave a huge sigh, and his eyes closed. "I thought you were coming to kill me," he said.

Slocum opened the man's blood-stained jacket. Blood and a brown liquid smelling of feces seeped from a wound in his right lower abdomen. "Help me, please," the Mexican asked.

Slocum shook his head. "A bullet went through your gut. Nothing I can do," he said.

The Mexican dragoons erupted from behind a row of trees under the cover of smoke and dust and galloped to the south, beyond the trees. An officer mounted on a great white stallion was in the lead. Slocum ran like a madman, dodged dead Mexicans, and leaped over boulders. It was no use; he could never catch up to the man on the white horse.

"*Ayúde me* [Help me]!" called the sergeant.

"Who is the man on the white horse?" Slocum asked.

The sergeant gasped and held a hand over his belly, "El Coronel, Don . . ." His eyes dimmed, and his head dropped to his shoulder. Slocum's mind whirled. This could be the white horse that carried away Billy Malone.

Abdominal wounds are always fatal, but if I can keep him alive, he might tell me the name of the rider, Slocum thought. The bullet had entered the abdomen just medial to the spine of the pelvic bone and exited through the muscles of the back. It must have gone through the first part of the large bowel. The best surgeons in Chicago and Europe had sutured holes in the bowel, but they worked in well-equipped operating rooms with trained assistants.

Soldiers carried the unconscious Mexican to the makeshift aid station. There was no morphine or ether and only an ounce or so of carbolic left in the saddlebags, but Slocum remembered cocaine was a local anesthetic. "Roll up your sleeves and scrub your hands," he said.

"You gonna try and save this damn Greaser?" Mulligan asked.

"He knows the name of the man who may have my friend." Slocum injected a mixture of cocaine and spring water around the wound. The patient didn't move when Slocum cut through the skin, fat, and muscles down to the peritoneum, the thin membrane that lined the abdominal cavity.

"Damn it, Mulligan, I can't see. Pull the muscles apart." The hole in the bowel, with pouting pink mucosa deep in the wound, was next to the appendix. Slocum gently pulled the injured bowel to the surface.

"Mulligan, I can't close the hole, but if we suture the bowel to the skin, the poison will drain to the outside and he won't get peritonitis," Slocum said.

"You mean he got to shit through the hole?" Mulligan said.

"Better than dying," Slocum said. He anchored the bowel to the skin with catgut sutures, swabbed the wound with the last of his carbolic, and hastily closed the muscles and skin. It was a rough job, some might call it butchery, but he had given the man a chance to live—and he might learn where to find Billy Malone.

Geronimo's warriors and the government scouts would have killed all the Mexicans, but Tom Horn talked them out of starting another war. The Apaches caught the Mexican horses and took guns, ammunition, and money from the dead.

Geronimo and Naiche, with fifteen warriors and grown boys followed by a crowd of women and children, rode into the American camp the day after the battle. Several women had babies in papoose pouches slung on their backs. The men carried Winchesters and had bandoliers of cartridges around their chest. The boys proudly brandished newly captured Mexican Remington rifles. Yanuza rode behind Geronimo on a high-spirited, dappled pony. He had a bow and quiver with arrows strapped to his back and a new rifle in hand. Das-Te-Sah was alone at the end of the crowd. The scar on her nose was a white line, and she no longer concealed her face. There was pride in her step when she walked up to Dr. Slocum. "You gave me a new life," she said.

The Mexican sergeant had a shaking chill on the evening of the second day and burned with fever all night. In the morning, thin yellow pus drained from the swollen, red wound. It was not the thick white "laudable" pus that doctors thought meant normal healing before the days of antisepsis, but the type of drainage that meant death within a few hours. Slocum found Das-Te-Sah stirring a pot of stew over a small fire.

"I need your help," Slocum said.

She immediately followed the doctor to the wounded sergeant. The medicine woman bent close to the wound and sniffed the fetid drainage. "Have a pot of boiling water ready when I return," she said.

Without a word, she disappeared over the ridge toward a small creek. She returned within an hour and dropped a double handful of roots into the simmering pot. The mixture developed a white froth, and the liquid became viscous as the mixture boiled down. When it suited her, she removed the pot from the fire to cool. She touched the catgut stitches with the point of her knife. "Bah, these hold in the poison." With an upward flick of the blade, she cut the stitches.

The wound fell open, revealing a dirty membrane covering the muscles. She poured a small measure of the potion into the wound and quickly covered the skin with clean white buckskin. Next, she pulled hot pebbles from the fire with wooden tongs and carefully placed each hot stone on the buckskin and piled on more buckskin. "Heat draws the poison," she said. Das-Te-Sah repeated the process twice during the day. The sergeant had one more shaking chill, and the fever persisted. His skin was ashen gray, hot to the touch. He batted the air with his hands, stared at the sky with frightened eyes, and cried out a woman's name. There was no pain when Slocum pressed on his abdomen. That meant the infection had not spread into the abdominal cavity; there was no peritonitis.

Das-Te-Sah forced broth, spoon by spoon, between the Mexican's lips. Most of it dribbled away, but after the first bowl he swallowed. On the fourth day, he opened his eyes; gas and liquid squirted out the bowel opening.

"Who is the man on the white horse?" Slocum asked. The Mexican sergeant looked at the sky with frightened, wandering eyes and clenched his teeth.

Captain Crawford never woke up and died on the fifth day. Lieutenant Maus wrapped the Tall Captain's body in a blanket while the Apache scouts sang a mournful death chant for their dead friend.

Maus sent a courier to General Crook with news of Geronimo's capture, the Mexican attack, and Crawford's murder. "It is time to return to Fort Bowie," he said.

The renegade Indians had respected Crawford's honesty and were saddened by his death. Naiche was "Chief" of the band, but wily Geronimo, a shaman with great power, spoke to Maus. "Crawford is dead. I will talk only with General Crook. Tell the general I will meet him at Embudo Canyon in one month," Geronimo said.

Before the wild Apaches left, Das-Te-Sah ground wild seeds and dried juniper berries between two stones and boiled the mixture with bits of venison liver into a mush. "This will make him strong," she said. When she removed the white buckskin covering, the redness and swelling had gone, and buds of healthy red tissue sprouted from deep in the wound. She gave Slocum a clay pot filled with honey. "Pass the blade of a knife through flames, and with the blade, apply honey to the wound," she said.

Pete and Zeke strung a hammock between two gentle mules for the wounded Mexican and placed Crawford's body on a travois, pulled by his horse. The dispirited troop set off on a slow march to the north. At Nacori Chico, the first Mexican village, Lieutenant Maus had a proper coffin made for Crawford's body. Slocum and Mulligan sat by a small fire with their backs to a warm boulder. They covered the Mexican sergeant with blankets and propped him up to feed him mush. His eyes were sunken, and his body had dwindled to skin and bone.

"Look at me," Slocum said. The sergeant's eyes slowly opened and focused on Slocum's face. "Who was the man on the white horse?"

The sergeant made a great sigh and raised his hand to his face. "If I tell you, he will kill my family." His eyes closed but flickered open a moment later. His words, in Spanish, were slurred.

"Bring Tom Horn!" Slocum shouted. Horn arrived, spoke to the man in Spanish and interpreted.

"I have seen death. Only the Devil can hurt me now. May God strike me." The man's head lolled to one side, and spit drooled from his lips.

Horn shook his arm. "*Por favor, mas,*" the scout said.

Intestinal gas gurgling from the wound aroused the sergeant. "He is El Coronel, Don Diego Vincenzo Riviera de Paulo."

Tom Horn whistled between his teeth. "Oh, Jesus, save us," he said.

"Ask him, how can I find him?" Slocum asked.

"You don't want to find this man. He hates North Americans. Don Diego has an army that scours the country for men to work in his silver mines. He especially likes to enslave North Americans," Horn said.

"Please, ask him."

"*Dónde está Don Diego?*" The sergeant rolled his head and weakly batted the air with his hand. "Your doctor, the man who saved your life, must know," Horn said.

"He may be in his hacienda, but Don Diego is very rich and has houses in Mexico City and Havana, maybe even Spain."

"Where is his hacienda?"

"In the mountains near the river Yaqui," the sergeant whispered.

"Zeke, saddle Nelly. I am leaving now," Slocum said.

Mulligan knocked the ashes from his pipe and aimed the stem at Slocum. "Where you aimin' to go?" he asked.

"The river Yaqui. I will find the son of a bitch," Slocum growled.

"Doc, the Mexicans'll kill ye in a minute. Besides, half the men are pukin' their guts out from eatin' bad beef. You have a heap of doctorin' to do before we get to the fort," Mulligan said.

"You will need maps and an escort," Tom Horn said.

Slocum slumped and leaned his back against the boulder. "I guess you're right."

The troop followed the east branch of the Bavispe River, where the horses and mules found good grass and the men had fresh water. At each village, a detachment of Mexican soldiers rode out, rifles in hand, to taunt the Apache scouts. The scouts were outnumbered and grimly rode on without answering. At Bavispe, a Mexican captain drew his pistol on Lieutenant Maus.

"You have invaded my country. My men should kill the lot of you," he said.

The scouts and American soldiers loaded and cocked their rifles, but their bandoliers were nearly empty of cartridges. Before shooting started, a senior Mexican officer galloped from the town and ordered his men to their barracks. "We do not want another war with your country, but take the Indians and leave, pronto," he said. When tempers cooled, the officer told of the Apache's raids, killing ranchers, stealing cattle, and taking women hostage.

Each evening, Slocum studied Tom Horn's notebook and practiced Spanish with the sergeant, whose name was Manuel. The Mexican finished a bowl of mush and chewed dry corn-bread. "I feel strong enough to go with the army," he said.

"You can thank the Apache medicine woman," Slocum said.

Manuel gripped the doctor's hand. "Please, do not pursue Don Diego. He will force you to work in his mine until you die."

Near the middle of February, the troop made camp near Embudo Canyon, twelve miles from the border. There were daily reports of Apache raids on ranches and villages but no word from General Crook. A pack train from Fort Bowie brought supplies and reinforcements. Near the middle of March, fires burned in the mountains, and the scouts reported the Apaches were near. The next day, Geronimo and Naiche, with well-mounted warriors, women, and children, rode into camp with a herd of horses and cattle. Slocum watched the Apaches sweep through the camp like a proud conquering army rather than a beaten-down rabble. They had new blankets and plenty of ammunition as a result of their raids. The Indians made camp a mile away from the Americans in a canyon with good water and close to mountains if they needed to run and hide.

Lieutenant Maus sent flour, sugar, and coffee to the Indians, but Geronimo refused to talk to anyone but Crook. The general, with his entourage of officers, arrived a week later and imme-diately arranged a council with the hostile Indians. Crook sat on a log beneath a cottonwood tree. The officers, men, and the Apache scouts formed a semicircle behind the general. Slocum and Mulligan edged near the front of the group. The Apache warriors, with long knives in their belts and Winchesters in the crooks of their arms, stood a few yards away. Geronimo approached Crook with his arms folded over his rifle. He made no greeting but spoke rapidly and urgently. Tom Horn inter-preted Geronimo's lengthy speech.

"My people left the reservation because white men never keep promises. You tell us to plant seeds and learn to farm but put us on worthless land that will grow nothing. The agents cheat and tell us not to drink beer. The white men in Arizona say I should hang from a tree. That is not right." Geronimo gripped his rifle and continued speaking until sweat poured down his face. Crook's face remained hard as steel. He looked at the ground and said not a word. When Geronimo finished his speech, Crook pointed at the shaman.

"Your mouth talks too many ways. You lie too many times," Crook said. When Horn translated his words, the Indians shook their weapons and shouted. The Americans reached for their guns.

The sound of pounding hooves and cries of "Yippy! Yippy!" broke the tension. Ulzana, with a half dozen warriors, drove a herd of cattle and horses through the Americans and on to the Indian camp. Geronimo said not a word, but Chihuahua, a chief with Ulzana, suddenly walked up to Crook and extended his hand.

"My heart has changed. We can all be brothers," he said. He and Crook shook hands.

The general faced Geronimo and the hostiles. "You must surrender and return to the reservation. If you stay on the warpath, I will kill every one of you if it takes fifty years. Go to your camp and think of my words. Choose death, or peace and life with your families," Crook said.

Mulligan, Pete, and Zeke snored in their bedrolls, but Tom Slocum watched the coals of a dying fire and listened to the drumbeats and chanting from the Indian camp. There were occasional bursts of gunfire when the Indians emptied their rifles at the night sky. Slocum sighted over his cupped right hand at the moon, which was indented on the left side. It was a bright waxing moon. Tom had never seen the stars so bright. He thought of long kisses with Rachel during buggy rides under the stars.

There was no sound, only a shadow, a touch on his shoulder, and a soft voice. "It is I, Das-Te-Sah."

She folded her skirt and sat down, leaning near Slocum. "What will become of my people?" she asked.

Slocum gazed at the ash-covered coals and hesitated to give a truthful answer. At last he sighed. "General Crook would send them back to the reservation, but the white men in Washington will lock them behind bars in Florida for their crimes," Slocum said.

"Will we never see the sky and feel the wind?" she asked.

"Perhaps for only two years, but maybe more."

"My people will die. Is there no hope?" she asked.

"You must trust General Crook," Slocum said.

The next day, at noon, Geronimo and his chiefs rode into camp and dismounted in front of Crook's tent.

Chihuahua and Naiche surrendered first. Geronimo, stolid and unsmiling, was the last. "I have moved about the land, free as the wind. Now, my heart is yours. We want to see our wives and children again," he said. The soldiers burst into a cheer, and General Crook was happy. He had, after much bloodshed, accomplished his goal. The Arizona Territory would no longer fear the Indian menace.

That night, an unscrupulous trader sold fifteen gallons of whisky to the Indians. Their shouts, gunfire, and pandemonium lasted all night. The Americans slept with loaded rifles, but the Indians were too drunk to attack. In the morning, hungover Indians sprawled in their own vomit. Crook left, as planned, after giving orders to his officers to bring the Indians to Fort Bowie as soon as possible. The Apaches did not leave camp that day. Along with selling whisky, the trader had spread a rumor that the white men would kill all the Apaches. Before dawn the next day, Slocum heard the tinkle of a bell horse trotting away to the mountains. Geronimo and Naiche's people vanished. He wondered if Das-Te-Sah had warned Geronimo of prison in Florida. The people with Chihuahua and Ulzana went with the American column to Fort Bowie.

CHAPTER FIFTEEN
General Crook Resigns

The entire garrison lined up to pay their respects to the fallen Captain Crawford when the battered column rode into Fort Bowie at the beginning of April. The scouts escorted the sullen, dejected band of Apaches to a camp a mile from the fort. They had surrendered peacefully and had expected to return to the reservation, but two days after they arrived at the fort, troopers surrounded the Indians and took their weapons. They did not leave them with even a butcher knife to cut food. Slocum watched with dismay when soldiers herded the Indians on a train that would take them to prison in Florida and a life of disease and death.

Zeke rushed across the parade ground and burst into sick bay. "Doc, you heard the news? Crook has resigned. The whole territory and them bigwigs in Washington blame him for lettin' Geronimo go loose," Zeke said.

"That's right. General Nelson Miles is taking his place," Mulligan said.

The sergeant raised his right hand and flexed his fingers. "Doc, I kin shoot as good as ever, thanks to you. The new captain said I can go back to my squad, so I will be leaving you."

"My time is up. As soon as I collect my money from the army, I am leaving for Mexico to find my friend," Slocum said.

"You aren't goin' to find nothin' but trouble," Mulligan replied.

Zeke hung his head and shuffled his feet. "Doc, you been awful good to me, but I done joined the army and will be in Sergeant Mulligan's squad," Zeke said.

"Good for you. The army is an honorable profession. I aim to go find Billy Malone," Slocum said.

General Crook would leave in the morning. It was a fine warm evening for his last sunset dress parade. Officers turned out wearing spiked and gold-tasseled shakos, blue jackets with gold braid, and striped trousers. The enlisted men lined up in their best and cleanest uniforms and, afterward, gave a concert while General and Mrs. Crook rested in rocking chairs on the front porch. The brass band played the old tunes, and as soldiers always do, the men began to sing. First was "The Battle Hymn of the Republic," and then a soldier with a clear tenor voice sang a solo:

Mid pleasures and palaces though we may roam,
Be it ever so humble, there is no place like home.

Slocum was not the only one who wiped away a tear when the last note of "Home Sweet Home" lingered in the dusk. The buffalo soldiers took up a slow, mournful version of "Go Down Moses" and then,

Michael row de boat ashore, Hallelujua.
Michael boat a gospel boat, Hallelujua.
I wonder where my Mudder deh,
See my Mudder on a rock, gwine home.

The tune had scarcely died away when the band struck up a Southern tune, and half the garrison sang out.

Come brothers, rally for the right.
The bravest of the brave
Sends his ringing battle cry.
Come rally round the blue flag
That bears a single star.
Hurrah! Hurrah! For Southern rights, hurrah!

Most of the men cheered, but there were a few boos. All joined in the comic song:

Come on, come old man,
And don't be made a fool.
I'll tell you as best I can,
John Morgan stole your mule.

The fellows repeated the last line, saying, "No, Old Geronimo stole your mule."

The men stood and gathered before the general and his wife for the last song.

We are tenting tonight on the old campground.
Give us a song to cheer our weary hearts,
A song of home and friends we love so dear.

Tom Horn fell in beside Slocum for the walk back to the officer's quarters. "Hear you are going to Mexico. Don't tangle with Don Diego. He will kill you if the peons don't do you in first. Wear a good frock coat, claim you are looking for a place to practice and you want to invest in mining. It won't hurt to say you are English or German. They hate us Americans," Horn said.

"That is good advice. What is the best route to the Yaqui River?" Slocum asked.

Horn quickly sketched a map in Slocum's notebook. "Follow the right fork of the Bavispe River south," Horn said.

General Miles lost no time in blaming Crook's reliance on Apache scouts for his failure to capture Geronimo. "American cavalry will do the job," he said. Miles brought in his own officer staff and a new regular army surgeon.

Tom Slocum bought a new black frock coat, gray trousers, a vest, string tie, and new boots at the company store. As he tried on the new coat, his eyes lit on a black hat with a narrow brim and low crown. It looked European or at least Eastern. "You do indeed appear to be a professional man," the clerk said.

The next morning, after rounds on his patients, he packed instruments and a few medical supplies into a canvas bag. A new officer, in a spotless uniform with bright new lieutenant's stripes, bounded into sick bay. He was over six feet and had a bushy mustache and thinning hair parted in the middle and slicked down on both sides of his head. "What can I do for you?" Slocum asked.

"I am Lieutenant Leonard Wood, the new medical officer."

Slocum rose and offered his hand. The lieutenant struck a pose. "I expect a salute, not a handshake. Have the patients ready for inspection; they are to stand at attention."

"These men are sick and need their rest," Slocum said.

"Soldiers need discipline," Wood replied. Men with leg wounds, dysentery, and pneumonia rose from their cots and did their best to stand straight, with eyes forward. One poor fellow fell in a dead faint.

Wood paced between the row of cots, frowning as he went. "These fellows need exercise, some close-order drill," he said. Wood strutted back to the office. Slocum shambled along behind.

"Doctor, you had best check the supplies. We are out of carbolic antiseptic and low on ether," Slocum said.

"Balderdash! My Harvard professors didn't believe in germs. I don't use carbolic or any other antiseptic hokum," Wood replied.

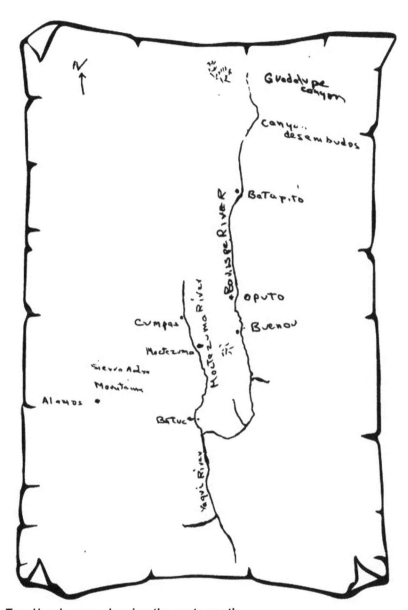

Tom Horn's map, showing the route south

CHAPTER SIXTEEN
A Perilous Road South

Nelly, rested and well-fed, stepped out at an easy trot along the familiar trail to Guadalupe Canyon. Tom Slocum would have felt more comfortable in his worn canvas breeches and a flannel shirt. The black coat gave him an air of professional respectability and hid the old Colt .32-20 that he carried in a belt holster. He hoped he wouldn't need the gun but had done a lot of target practice, just in case. When Nelly shied at a buzzing rattlesnake, Slocum took its head off with the first shot.

He ended the first, long day at the San Bernardino Ranch, a spread operated by an American couple a few miles north of the border. The rancher saw him coming from a long way off and gave a shout when Slocum came even with the windmill. "Hi, stranger. What can I do for you?"

"A place to sleep and supper," Slocum said.

"Sure thing. I am Bill Doyle. Sam will take your horse."

"Seen any Indians?" Slocum asked.

"Nary a one," Doyle replied.

"Crook just about had them licked, but Geronimo is still on the loose," Tom said. He tilted his hat to the petite blonde woman who met him at the door.

"Dr. Tom Slocum at your service, ma'am," he said.

"I am Betty. There is a cot in the lean-to, and I will get a basin of water so you can wash up."

Dinner in the cheerful log cabin was fried chicken, biscuits, gravy, beans baked with molasses, and bread pudding The two boys, Sam and Charley, did not say a word but gawked at Slocum's fine new suit.

"I haven't eaten this well since leaving home. How can I repay you?" Slocum asked.

"Would you mind looking at Charley? His shoulder ain't been right since a bronco threw him last week."

The boy was about fifteen years old, skinny but tough. "What happened?" Slocum asked.

"I was breakin' a new horse. When he tossed, I landed on my arm," Charley said. His left arm was held away from his body, and he winced when Slocum touched the shoulder joint and felt the head of the humerus out of place.

"Can you stand a little pain for a few minutes?" Slocum asked.

"Damn right," Charley said.

"Lay on the floor, on your back." Slocum shucked off his left boot and placed his stocking foot in Charley's armpit. "Now, you just relax while I pull on your arm," Slocum said. It took nearly ten minutes of constant traction before the head of the humerus slipped into place with an audible *pop*.

"Wear this sling and bandage for two weeks. If you don't, it will pop out again," Slocum said.

Slocum filled up on bacon and eggs and was on the trail before the sun peaked over the Peloncillo Mountains. He checked his compass and figured he had crossed the unmarked boundary between Mexico and the United States by ten o'clock. He moseyed along, keeping Nelly to a walk, while he watched the red cliffs and brushy canyons for Apaches or Mexicans.

Just before dusk, he reached a creek that, according to Tom Horn's map, should be the headwaters of the Bavispe River. Nelly was ankle-deep in the cold rushing waters when her ears flicked; she raised her head and whinnied. Slocum listened, but there was only the sound of water riffling over rocks and cottonwood leaves whispering in a light breeze. He raised Nelly's head and turned her to the shore. There in the shadows were two figures. Tom sat back in the saddle and remained still.

"It is I, Das-Te-Sah." The Apache woman moved into the light on a small, mouse-colored mule. Yanuza followed on a splendid gray stallion with white stockings on each forefoot.

His bow and a quiver of arrows were strapped to his back; he carried a rifle across the crook of his left arm, and bandoliers of cartridges crisscrossed his naked chest. The saddle was of embossed leather with silver trim. A young antelope was slung behind the saddle. His face was set in a hard frown, but the gun was not pointed at Slocum.

"We went with Geronimo, but he has taken his warriors on the fighting path and left the young men to protect the women and children. He left us to watch for the American army." Das-Te-Sah's voice rose. "You white people lie to us. We will never go on the black train," she said.

"I am no longer with the army but am seeking my friend. I want to be your friend. That is a fine horse and saddle."

"I took the horse and the rifle from Mexicans after they killed the Tall Captain," Yanuza said.

"The Mexicans will kill you. The new American general has offered fifty dollars for Apaches, dead or alive, and he has many troops. You are doomed," Slocum said.

"You leave us alone, go away from this place," the woman said.

Slocum got down from his horse. "I had planned to camp here. "Let us be friends and share our food," he said.

While Yanuza skinned and butchered the antelope, the woman started a fire by inserting a stick into a hollowed-out bit of wood and spun the stick between the palms of her hands until a wisp of smoke appeared. She put the glowing ember in a handful of bark and blew until the tinder burst into flames. When fire burned down to coals, she put on a pot of water and dumped a mixture of ground acorns, piñon nuts, and wild seeds from a buckskin bag into the water. Slocum added a double handful of dried beans and a chunk of brown sugar. Das-Te-Sah roasted the antelope loin over the coals. When it was ready, Slocum scooped the gruel and a hunk of meat onto a tin plate from his mess kit and wolfed down the food. The Apaches ate with their fingers. Slocum made coffee with sugar, and then the woman tossed a handful of dry sticks on the coals. In the light of the flames, Slocum saw despair on the faces of the Indians. "I may be able to help you, but you must change your ways," he said.

"You whites always say you will help, but you lie," Das-Te-Sah said.

"I had both of you under my knife and you live."

"Yes, that is true." There was a long silence until she asked, "How can you help us?"

"I am traveling deep into Mexico to find my friend. You could be my servant. Yanuza can care for the horses and be my bodyguard. You must become Mexican."

"Bah, we Apaches hate Mexicans," she said.

"Your dress looks Mexican. Cut Yanuza's hair; he must wear Mexican clothing and learn Spanish words," Slocum said.

She translated for Yanuza, who beat his chest with his fist and shouted, "I am Apache, never, never a Mexican! If I cut my hair, Usan will not know me if I die."

"In your heart you will always be Apache, but you can learn new things and become a better Apache," Slocum said.

In the morning, Yanuza saddled the horses while the woman reheated last night's supper. "We have decided to follow you," she said. Yanuza hacked off handfuls of his shoulder-length hair with a bone-handled knife made from a US cavalry saber.

"You are now Pedro, and Das-Te-Sah is Maria. Say your names," Slocum said.

At noon, they came to a village of shabby adobe houses at the fork of the river. They left Yanuza in a brushy ravine. Slocum and Das-Te-Sah rode through a gate in the adobe wall into the village. Chickens scratched in the dusty street, and a dog with his head on his paws dozed in a sunny spot by the small plaza. Slocum and Das-Te-Sah dismounted at the door of a cantina. "Wait here," Slocum said.

The ceiling was low, the floor was dirt, and the two tables by a fly-specked window were empty. A man behind the bar, with a huge drooping mustache, looked up from a yellowed newspaper and rolled his one eye. "Americano?"

"No, English," Slocum said. He sat on a rickety stool at the bar and put down a silver dollar. "*Cerveza, por favor. Comidas* [Beer, please. Food]?" he asked.

"*Si, puerco y frijoles* [Yes, pork and beans]," the bartender said.

"*Dos platos* [Two dishes]." Slocum drank the warm, bitter beer, and when the bartender put the plates on the bar, he took one to Das-Te-Sah. "*Mi serviente* [My servant]," he said. The pork was tough and stringy, and the beans, covered with a red sauce, burned his tongue, but he ate everything.

"*Hable* English?" Slocum asked.

"*Un poco*," the bartender replied.

"Is there a store in the village?" Slocum asked.

The bartender pointed across the street. "*La tienda*, the woman has things to sell," he said.

"Have you seen Indians?" Slocum asked.

"They came and killed the men and took our women."

"Is it safe to travel? I hope to invest in silver mining."

"You have money?"

"Yes, money to invest in mines. I hope to meet with a man named Don Diego Vincenzo Riviera de Paulo," Slocum said.

The bartender rolled one eye and struck the bar with his fist. "*Dios Mio*. Get out. Go away from here. We have enough trouble."

Das-Te-Sah purchased baggy cotton pants, a shirt, and a broad-brimmed sombrero for Yanuza, a scarf for herself, corn meal, and beans at the small tienda.

With a look of loathing on his face, Yanuza put on clothing fit for a Mexican peon. "Burn the Apache clothing and the bow," Slocum said. Yanuza shouted in Apache and beat his fists on his chest in a storm of protest.

"He is right. If they found the Apache clothing, they would kill you," Das-Te-Sah said. The breechclout, leggings, and hair band went up in a cloud of smoke, but Yanuza wrapped the bow and quiver in a blanket tied to his saddle. He slung his bone-handled knife in a buckskin sheath with a thong over his shoulder.

"It will do," Slocum said.

The trail led away from the river to higher ground and through a narrow defile between a jumble of boulders, with the peaks of the Sierras on their right.

Less than a mile from the village, three men blocked the way. A squat man with a round, scarred face astride a mule held a long-barreled rifle on Slocum. The other two banditos, stocky men with wolfish grins, waved big revolvers from Yanuza to Slocum to the woman.

The man with the rifle pushed his sombrero back and adjusted the blanket over his shoulder. "The money, the woman, and the fine horse," he said.

Slocum opened his coat and then raised both hands, palm forward. "You can have the money, but leave the woman," he said. Das-Te-Sah's mule made a soft bray and stepped forward to nuzzle the Mexican's mount as if they were old friends. The scar-faced man shifted his gun to the woman. Yanuza's arm was a blur of motion. His bone-handled knife struck the man's skull behind the ear. "Ahh," he said. His mouth was still open when he slid to the ground. His hand, in death, convulsively closed on the trigger. The slug blasted a hole in the dirt, and the horses and mules reared. Without thinking, Slocum pulled his pistol and downed the bandit on his left with two quick shots. Yanuza blew the third bandito off his horse with one rifle blast. Slocum's man fell backward and lay on the ground, with his eyes and mouth wide open, as blood leaked out the two holes in his chest. He died with blood gurgling in his throat as he took his last breath of air. Slocum threw down his pistol and stroked the dead man's hand as if he could will him back to life.

"Oh God, I did not intend to kill him," Slocum murmured.

"You did what any man would do. He would have killed us both. You saved my life and yours," the Indian woman said.

Yanuza looked at Slocum with respect. "You are now a warrior as well as a healer," Das-Te-Sah said.

Slocum's face hardened. He put the pistol back in the holster and stood with his hand on the pommel of the saddle. "When the bandits don't return to the village, the militia will come for us. We must be far away. It is not proper for a peon to have such a fine horse and saddle. Everyone will know it was stolen. I will take the gray stallion, and Yanuza will ride my horse," Slocum said.

Yanuza slid off his fine horse and offered the reins to Slocum. He then picked up the long-barreled rifle. "It is a buffalo gun," he said.

"Yes, a Sharps. It will shoot a mile," Slocum said. Yanuza wrapped the rifle in a blanket with his bow.

The doctor consulted his compass and pointed to the southwest through a jumble of rocks, low trees, and a barren desert toward mountain peaks. "They will expect us to follow the river, so we will go to the mountains," Slocum said.

Yanuza led the way, keeping to rocky ledges where the horses left no traces. The woman came last and, with a bundle of twigs, swept their prints from patches of sand. They made camp after dark in a deep ravine with a small spring of clear water. In the morning, Yanuza climbed a peak and looked back over their trail. There were no followers. Slocum turned to the east, and that evening they again sighted the Bavispe River but stayed on high ground.

"That is the village of Oputo," the woman said. Her sharp eyes had spotted a collection of low adobe buildings in the valley next to the river. Slocum squinted into the dusty haze and finally found a church spire in the distance. In the morning, they rode into the valley on a road that led between fields of beans and corn with willow-lined irrigation ditches. The sizable village was surrounded by an adobe wall, but a gate opened onto a well-beaten road that led to a cool, shaded plaza with the church on one side and a cantina on the other. The riders stopped by a bubbly fountain that cascaded water into a pool surrounded by benches.

Slocum dismounted, sloshed water on his face, washed his hands, and took a long drink. The woman and Yanuza waited until he was finished, then drank and gave water to the horses and the mule. Chickens scratched in the dirt. Two brown and black dogs, one with a torn ear, rose on their haunches, woofed a warning, and settled down with their heads on paws. The only visible citizen was a peon covered with a serape asleep on the ground in front of the cantina. The Indians tied the animals to a rail in front of the cantina while Slocum settled on a bench by the fountain and stretched. At first, there was no sound, but he drowsed and either imagined or heard singing. When the hymn ended, old men and women with children streamed from the church. The people gazed at the strangers for a moment, then went their way toward the low adobe houses with covered porches that lined the dusty street.

Slocum was about to go to the cantina when a small boy, leading an elderly priest wearing a brown cassock belted with a rope, emerged from the church. The boy led the old man to a bench near Slocum and placed a small dish of breadcrumbs in his hands. "Gracias," the priest said. The boy glanced at the American, then skipped down the street. The priest tossed crumbs to the ground, and before long there was a flutter of wings. Cooing pigeons landed and pecked at the crumbs.

Slocum coughed and cleared his throat. The priest slowly turned halfway and looked directly at the doctor. There was a fringe of white hair around a bald spot on his head. His eyes were opaque with cataracts. Slocum realized he was totally blind. He could not think of the right Spanish words.

"Excuse me, Father. I hope I am not intruding," Slocum said in English.

"You are welcome to enjoy the sun and listen to the water make music. What is an American doing in our small village?" the priest asked.

"I am passing through, looking for a lost friend. How do you happen to speak English?" the doctor asked.

"I was in Tucson, when that city was a part of our country. When the Americans arrived, I learned English, but as my sight faded, I could no longer care for my flock. The bishop assigned me to this small village. I am Father Alonzo."

"An operation to remove the cataracts would restore your sight," Slocum said.

"I pray every day for a miracle, but in this village, there are no doctors."

"The operation is not difficult," Slocum said.

"Could it be done here?" asked the priest.

Slocum hesitated while the priest continued to feed crumbs to the pigeons. He felt somehow closer to Billy Malone and wanted to get on with the search for his friend, but didn't he have a duty to heal?

"If there is a place with good light in the morning, and if you can lie completely still, I could do the operation. It may or may not restore your sight."

"If only I can see the faces of my people and the morning sun, I would be happy. Lead me through the church. There is a suitable place where the morning sun shines brightly."

"My servants must come with me," Slocum said.

"They are welcome."

Inside, the church was cool and dark. The rough adobe walls were painted a dull brown, and there was one small stained-glass window. Slocum stopped before a small, crude statue at one side of the pulpit and, for a moment, held his breath in total awe.

Father Alonzo placed his hands on the statue. "She is the Virgin of Guadalupe, our own Virgin Mary," said Father Alonzo.

Her skin was dark, but her features were delicate, and straight black hair descended to her shoulders. The statue's hands were clasped as if in prayer, and a blue robe hung from her shoulders to the ground. "The original woman was a poor peasant. Centuries ago she had performed miracles, spoke in the native Indian language, and said she was the Virgin Mary. The Indians thought she was an Aztec goddess. The Spanish did not believe the story, but the dark virgin is the basis for Catholicism in the New World. I will pray to her for your success," Father Alonzo said.

Das-Te-Sah bowed to the statue. "The Virgin has great power, even for Apaches." She and Yanuza hobbled the animals in a small field behind the church and made their beds in the stable. Slocum followed the old priest to his simple but spotlessly clean adobe hut behind the church. An elderly mestizo nun with a crop of black hairs on her upper lip cooked their evening meal, which they took in a walled courtyard between the priest's quarters and the church.

In the false dawn of early morning, Slocum woke to Father Alonzo's murmured prayers. He prepared the instruments and instructed Das-Te-Sah on how to assist with the operation. At ten in the morning, when the sun provided good light, Father

Alonzo lay on the dinner table with his hands folded over his chest.

The sharpest bistoury, forceps, and a small hook fresh from a basin of boiling water lay on a carbolic-soaked towel, close at hand. "Hold his eyelid open," the doctor said.

Das-Te-Sah delicately separated the old priest's wrinkled eyelids. "Remain perfectly still," Slocum said. The priest's opaque eyes gazed heavenward while Slocum dropped a solution of cocaine into each eye. He waited a minute before making a small cut in the sclera, held the incision open with a small hook, then grasped the lens with the slender forceps. The lens came out with a gentle tug and a twist.

"Close your left eye," Slocum said. He quickly folded a pad over the eye and wrapped a bandage around the priest's head.

"Are you ready for the second eye?" Slocum asked.

"I saw a flash of light. Yes, do the other eye," Father Alonzo said. He removed the second cataract as easily as the first, but the doctor's hands trembled when he applied the second bandage.

"You must lie absolutely still for two days and keep both eyes bandaged for a week," the doctor said.

Four men from the village carried the old priest to his bed in the darkened room. Slocum was by his bedside when the priest awakened from a nap, late that afternoon. It was a good sign that fluid had not drained from the eyeballs. "Father, you may have the answer to my quest for a dear friend," Slocum said.

"I will help you if I can," the priest replied.

"Do you know of Don Diego Vincenzo Riviera de Paulo?"

Father Alonzo struggled and tried to rise. Slocum put his hands on the priest's chest. "Father, you must lie still."

"That man is evil. His men come every year to take our strongest boys. They never return."

"Where does he take them?"

"The people whisper about a black mountain made of pure silver where Don Diego has a mine."

"Where?" Slocum asked.

For a moment the priest scarcely breathed, and then his voice was a gentle sigh. "You must not go there."

John Raffensperger, MD

"I must."

"If you insist on going to your death, follow the river until the waters join to form the Yaqui River, then face the setting sun. The black mountain is three days' journey across a desert and two mountains," said Father Alonzo.

CHAPTER SEVENTEEN

The Black Mountain

The old nun filled their saddlebags with cornmeal and dried beans. They set out when it was still dark, traveled all day, and that evening waded into bubbling, clear water at the head of the Yaqui River. The horses and the mule drank their fill. Yanuza filled skin water bags and Slocum's canteens.

The Indian woman shaded her eyes and faced the sun, an orange ball hanging over the Sierras. "The ancients said the black mountain spit fire and smoke, and many people died. Near the mountain, the springs give hot water that tastes bad, and even the air smells of an evil spirit. The old ones would not go near the mountain, and the grandmothers never spoke the name," Das-Te-Sah said.

In the morning they crossed a great sand dune where there was no water, and the horses sunk to their fetlocks in loose sand. Yanuza went ahead, and just as the sun disappeared over the mountains, he found a small seep of water, hardly more than wet sand, in a canyon at the foot of the mountains. They ate beans on cornmeal cakes the Mexicans called "tortillas" and gnawed meat from the bones of a rabbit.

Yanuza led the way up and down canyons and across narrow trails on the sides of mountains. Slocum held the reins loosely and let the gray stallion find his way. The horse was sure-footed and did not falter, even when he touched bare rock, while a thousand-foot precipice fell away on the other side of the path. Slocum shut his eyes and let the horse find its way.

On the third day, Das-Te-Sah pointed to a sharp peak and a wisp of smoke outlined against a clear blue sky. "The black mountain has fire inside," she said. That night, they made camp in a grove of stunted pine trees a mile away from the base of the mountain. They had no fire but ate cold beans and drank the dregs from their canteens because the water that bubbled up from a small spring was warm and tasted of sulfur.

"We are near the enemy," Das-Te-Sah said. During the night, Slocum awoke to see Yanuza pacing like a cat, rifle at the ready, but they were not disturbed. In the morning, Das-Te-Sah stayed hidden in the grove with the horses while Yanuza and Slocum crept through the trees to a rocky outcrop near the base of the black mountain. When the first rays of sunshine fell on the gray lava rocks that covered the small valley, Slocum made out low buildings, a wooden derrick, and a line of ox carts. Soon, men emerged from the nearest building and disappeared into a black, cave-like opening at the base of the mountain. Without a word, Yanuza slipped off his white shirt and baggy pants, and with only his knife, he slithered away between the lava rocks. His dark skin blended with the sand; in the blink of an eye, he had disappeared from sight. Men with rifles came from a second building next to a horse corral. All through the day, men emerged from the mine entrance staggering under huge loads that they dumped in the carts. In the afternoon, the train of carts, drawn by teams of oxen and escorted by men on horseback, lumbered across the valley to the southeast.

Slocum waited through the day, sucking on a pebble to relieve his thirst. Night came on suddenly, still with no sign of Yanuza. Slocum looked to the northwest for familiar constellations. The North Star was just visible over the mountain, the Little Dipper stood on its handle, and the tail of the Big Dipper pointed to bright Arcturus high in the sky when Slocum felt Yanuza's light touch. They returned to the horses and Das-Te-Sah. The woman gave them the last of the dry tortillas and brackish water.

Das-Te-Sah translated for Yanuza. "He says the workers are locked in a strong building with bars on the windows. One of the men is a tall, dark-haired gringo who has iron shackles on his legs. At night, two men with rifles guard the strong building, but they drink the mescal and fall asleep."

Yanuza drew his finger across his neck. "I can kill them both."

The woman wrapped the horses' hooves in pieces of blanket, and they led the animals through the shadow of the mountain. Yanuza crept forward and did his work on the sleeping guards with his bone-handled knife. Yanuza made a single yip of a coyote; Slocum slipped silently to the side of the Indian. The guard's heads were nearly severed from their bodies, and the ring of keys was sticky with blood. Slocum fumbled at the lock until a key opened the heavy iron door that led to a large room filled with sleeping prisoners. Yanuza stood guard while the doctor lit a single candle. At the light, a peon groaned. Slocum clapped his hand over the man's mouth.

"*Dónde está el gringo* [Where is the gringo]?" he asked.

The man rolled his eyes and pointed to a dim corridor. "*Ustedes, vamoos sin ruido* [You, leave without noise]," Slocum said. The prisoners picked themselves up from the dirt floor and fled.

The corridor led to a barred cell with a man sprawled on the floor.

"Billy, Billy Malone?" Slocum said. The man with a shaggy beard lifted his head. "Billy, it's me, Tom."

"Tom, is it really you?" Slocum opened the cell with another brass key and extended his hand to Malone.

"You are free. Let's go," Slocum whispered.

"My feet are shackled and chained to the wall, Malone said.

A padlock connected the shackle to an iron chain that ran through a bolt on the wall. None of the keys fit the brass padlock. "It will be light soon. You best get out of here," Billy said.

"No, damn it. We go together," Slocum said. He raised the old Colt and took aim at the shackle.

"No, the noise will bring the guards," Billy said. Slocum fired from a foot away. The padlock shattered, and in a moment he had loosened the chains, but Billy could hardly get to his feet. Tom and Yanuza half carried and half dragged Billy to the door.

The moon was down, but the first faint light of a false dawn outlined distant mountains. Yanuza signaled Das-Te-Sah with a coyote yip. Coyotes answered from the surrounding hills until the valley reverberated with yips and howls. A mule brayed in the guards' corral, and a man with his pants around his knees came from the door of the guards' barracks. Das-Te-Sah emerged from the shadows into the gray light, riding her mule and leading the two horses. Slocum mounted the gray stallion and tried to pull Billy Malone up behind the saddle. Billy's legs gave way and he collapsed. "Go on, I can't make it," he mumbled. Yanuza, with shear brute strength, heaved him on the horse behind Slocum.

"Hang on!" Slocum shouted. The three went at a gallop back across the lava field toward safety in the trees. Men poured out of the barracks and commenced firing. The stallion shuddered and stumbled when a bullet tore into his hindquarter. Das-Te-Sah dropped back and made a grab for Slocum and Billy but failed. She and Yanuza escaped to the trees in a fusillade of bullets.

The officer ordered his men to throw a rope over Tom and Billy and drag them back to a rough courtyard in front of the barracks. Billy's legs gave out; he fell and rose again on bare feet. Blood trickled from a deep cut on his forehead. The furious officer with a thick mustache brandished a long-barreled revolver in Slocum's face. "Dog, killing is too good for you." He spit. "My men will flog you to death."

A puff of smoke rose from an outcropping of rock more than five hundred yards away. A moment later, the *boom* of Yanuza's buffalo gun rolled over the valley. The officer, with a look of absolute disbelief, cupped his hands to catch blood and bits of liver that flowed in a bright stream from a huge hole in his upper abdomen. He dropped the pistol and slowly toppled to the ground. A second shot brought down another Mexican guard. The rest, confused and panicked, backed away as if the two gringos had a hidden guardian angel who dealt death from an impossible distance. While the guards milled about, Slocum tried to catch the officer's horse, but a sergeant in the uniform of a militiaman fired a shot that barely missed him.

"No tiré! Estoy un médico Anglais, un amigo de Don Diego Vincenzo Riviera de Paulo. No tiré [Don't shoot! I am an English doctor and a friend of Don Diego]!" he shouted.

The sergeant lowered his rifle and said, "Let El Coronel decide the bastards' fate."

Furious guards clubbed the gringos with the butts of their rifles and then tied them in the back of an ox cart. The cart, jolting over a rough road, slowly brought Slocum out of the depths of darkness. He tasted blood in his mouth and came fully awake to stabbing pains in every part of his body. Billy Malone was face down in the cart; blood dribbled from his mouth, and his skin was ashen. An hour or so later—or it could have been longer because the sun, a great orange ball, was sinking in the west—Slocum found the strength to look through the planks that enclosed the cart. They had left the scrub mesquite trees and cactus and were on a smooth road flanked by irrigation ditches that watered fields of corn and beans. Slocum struggled to sit up and cradled Billy Malone's head. His friend was still breathing but feverish and unconscious. Slocum stared back over the road that led away to the black mountain. It could have been an hallucination, but way back in the distant haze, were there two figures on horseback?

CHAPTER EIGHTEEN

Don Diego

The road passed a cluster of adobe huts around a plaza and a church with a caved-in roof. Next was a tall adobe wall with imbedded shards of glass. Two mummified corpses hanging from gallows on either side of the road were not welcoming. The guard who stood rigidly at attention outside the guardhouse motioned the cart through the spiked iron gate with a languid wave of his rifle. The cart lumbered down a road lined with paloverde trees, past a stately, sprawling two-story adobe building surrounded by a porch and shaded with desert oaks. Further on, the whitewashed stables, harness, and blacksmith shops were just as impressive as the main house. Caballeros wearing velvet jackets and white trousers tucked into shiny high leather boots worked high-stepping thoroughbred horses in an outdoor arena next to the stables.

Don Diego's wealth did not extend to the dank stone-walled cell with a single barred window. Slocum staggered from the cart on his own two feet but fell in a heap on the floor. The guards dragged Billy through manure and dirt, then tossed him onto a wooden cot. For a while, the cool rough stones felt good to Slocum's fevered body, but then he had a shaking chill and came awake to voices and the light of a lantern. A rough guard prodded Billy. "*Muerto por la mañana* [Dead by morning]," he said.

A strong guard grabbed a handful of Tom's hair, jerked Slocum to his feet, and dragged him by his manacled hands across the yard to the great adobe house. They entered a door that led to a brightly lit room with whitewashed walls. The guard hung the key ring on a hook by the door.

Spanish grandees, some with families, others on horseback, surveyed the room from somber oil paintings that left no doubt about Don Diego's royal lineage. The guards left Slocum swaying on his feet, facing a cruelly handsome man who did not look up from an exquisitely inlaid chessboard. Don Diego toyed with a white pawn carved from ivory. The black pieces nearest Slocum were ebony.

Don Diego had a jutting nose and a narrow, creased, aristocratic face. He had evidently spent a lot of time in the sun, but there was no trace of gray in his black, straight hair. He wore a snow-white shirt with frills and long cuffs, turned back to show his thick wrists covered with black hair. Don Diego's hand hovered over the board; he moved the white king's pawn two spaces forward.

Something deep inside Slocum came awake. He lifted the heavy cuff and chain over the board and with two dirty fingers moved the black king's pawn to the center space opposite the white pawn. Don Diego's lips curled, and his eyes opened wide. He moved the king's knight; Slocum followed with the black king's knight.

"I expected you would open with the Ruy Lopez, the Spanish Game," Slocum said in a slurred voice.

Don Diego glanced at Slocum and studied the chess pieces for several minutes. He finally spoke in clear, nearly unaccented but lazy English. "You are the American doctor who has been hounding me for many months. Now the fox has caught the hunter. I should hang your dirty neck, but you amuse me." Slocum took the Don's knight with a bishop with his fifth move, but Don Diego mated his king after twenty moves.

"You play well. I may let you live until you become boring," Don Diego said.

"I want only to take my friend home. We are of no consequence or danger to you," Slocum said.

"Who is this friend?"

"Lieutenant Malone."

Don Diego rose and spit in Slocum's face. "He was with the damn Indians who killed my men. The Yankee cur is my prisoner. You American dogs took our land by war and stole my father's mines in Arizona."

"Now we are your allies to capture the hostile Apaches who raid your villages," said Slocum.

"*Bebidas, pronto* [Drinks, now]!" shouted Don Diego. The woman who appeared from a side door with a bottle and a tall glass on a tray looked like an animal expecting a kick. Her head was turned to one side with her chin elevated, and her spine was crooked. Her hands trembled when she placed the tray on the table next to the chessboard.

"Stupid woman, be careful," Don Diego snapped.

The woman, with a small, well-formed hand, poured clear liquid into the tall glass. Don Diego tossed off the drink at one gulp. "*Más.*" She poured another drink for the Don. "Mescal. Pure, distilled mescal. Are you man enough to drink like a Mexican?"

Slocum nodded. "Then drink," the Don said. The first sip burned like the fires of Hades. Slocum waited a moment, then finished the glass. Flames leaped in his stomach and his brain reeled, but he kept to his feet while Don Diego tossed off another glass and smacked his lips.

When his head stopped spinning, Slocum paid closer attention to the woman. She was young, and her head was twisted so that her chin pointed up and to the right. Her eyes were slightly crossed, and her head was flattened on the left side. Slocum realized her twisted back was an attempt to keep her head and eyes level. Her features were regular, almost dainty. She had chestnut-colored hair and, aside from her twisted spine, had a comely figure. She was almost beautiful but was dressed plainly in a simple, gray blouse. Her riding skirt was split up the middle, like a full-cut man's trousers.

"Ha, you stare at my daughter, a damned cripple. No man will marry the homely bitch. Even the convent refused her. Look at her! She won't wear women's clothes and rides like a man. She cares more about horses than her own father."

Don Diego sent his glass crashing into the fireplace. "She was born cursed and killed my wife," the Don said.

"It is not a curse. She has a tight muscle in her neck that causes her head to turn. It is called torticollis and is easily cured with an operation," Slocum said.

"Pah, you Yankees stick together. Her mother was American. Get out of my sight and bring food," Don Diego said. The woman scurried away and returned with a silver plate filled with meat, smoked fish, steamed vegetables, and a small loaf of white bread.

A huge fireplace with a brisk fire was next to the table. English double-barrel shotguns and engraved rifles rested in glass cabinets, and a pearl-handled Colt revolver in a holster hung by a cartridge belt on a wall hook within Don Diego's reach. The Don finished eating and shoved the half-empty plate to Slocum. "The scraps are fit for a dog. Go on, eat," he said.

"My friend is sick. He needs food more than me," Slocum said.

"Guard!" Don Diego swept the plate to the floor. "Take the prisoner."

When the moon was down, Slocum awoke on the floor of the cell to the sound of a soft rustle. The cell door swung open. In the dim light of a shaded candle lantern, he made out the hunchbacked woman. At her side was an elderly Mexican with a copper pot. "Food for you and your friend," she said.

"Oh, the poor man." The woman lifted Billy Malone to a semi-sitting position and cradled him in her arms.

She wiped the blood and dirt from his face with a cloth soaked in warm water and bathed his eyes. Billy moaned, opened his eyes, and stared at the apparition. "Open your mouth," she said. Billy sucked in a spoon of broth, then more, and finally lay back with a sigh.

The old man offered the pot and a large spoon to Slocum. He tipped up the pot and drank the broth, then scooped the last bits of chicken with rice and beans.

"Thank you. What is your name?" he asked.

"Theresa."

"Is Don Diego really your father?"

"In name only. Damn his soul. He blames me for the death of my mother." She paused and then, with a timid catch in her voice, asked, "Can I really be cured with an operation?"

167

"I have seen the operation. It is simple, and afterward you would be normal," Slocum said.

She left a jug of water and blankets, then silently left. "I shall return tomorrow," she said.

The guards took Slocum to play chess with Don Diego at night. After the guards dragged him back to the cell, the woman brought food and cared for their wounds. On the third day, Billy managed a few steps and said, "Theresa said she would help us escape."

"She would have to be a magician," Slocum said.

That evening she crouched near Slocum and whispered into his ear, "He will soon tire of playing chess and will torture and murder both of you with his own hands."

"He has been pleasant the last few nights," Slocum said.

"He is a sadist and hates Americans. A woman who asks about two gringos is in the village. A boy who is nearly a man is with her," Theresa said.

Slocum rested his hand on Theresa's arm. "They are my friends. Tell them to find a hiding place and watch for us."

That night, Slocum won in forty moves. Don Diego swept the beautiful chess pieces to the floor. "Damn American dog. You cheated. I should kill you now."

"You watched every move. I did not cheat. Perhaps you don't feel well."

"Bah, Theresa, *bebidas.*" The Don took down the first glass of mescal at a gulp and offered the bottle to Slocum. Feigning clumsiness with his cuffed hand, Slocum spilled half the bottle. The almost-pure alcohol ran down the Don's leg and onto the floor. Slocum hurled the bottle into the fireplace and ducked behind the table. The bottle exploded in a ball of fire. A glass shard slashed through the Don's thigh, and a blue flame raced from the fireplace up his boots to his trousers. In a moment, flames enveloped the Don.

"No, ah, aheeee!" he screamed. Theresa rushed into the room, seized the key ring and unlocked Slocum's cuffs while the Don rolled on the floor and beat at the flames with his bare hands. The alcohol quickly burned out, leaving the Don's cloth-

168

ing smoldering. His face was blistered, his hair was singed, and blood ran from the wound in his thigh, but he was not seriously injured. The Don reached for the Colt pistol, but Slocum whirled the chain and struck the Don behind his ear. Theresa gave the Colt to Slocum.

"Finish him," she said.

"No, I can't do that." They bound Don Diego's mouth with the sleeve of his shirt and cuffed him to the table.

Slocum opened the gun case and grabbed a long, lever-action Winchester rifle and a handful of ammunition. "Let's go," he said.

Theresa had the horses saddled behind the stables. Billy Malone staggered from the cell to the horses and put a foot in the stirrup but didn't have the strength to swing over the saddle. Theresa pushed his leg up and over and put the reins in one hand. "Hold on to the pommel," she said.

"What about the guards?" Slocum asked.

"Take off your coat." She gave Slocum and Malone wide sombreros and leather vests. They resembled vaqueros. "Keep your heads down."

They approached the guardhouse at a slow walk. "*Señorita, qué pasa?*" the guard asked.

"*Pedro, está una noche buena, voy a montar en caballo con mis amigos* [Pedro, it is a nice night. I am going horseback riding with my friends]," Theresa answered.

The guard bowed. "*Va con Dios* [Go with God]," he said.

They were a dozen miles away, near the edge of the fields and the beginning of the desert; the moon, setting over mountains to the west, cast long shadows. Two riders stepped out from a cluster of willow trees alongside an irrigation ditch.

"We have watched you since the moon was high," Das-Te-Sah said.

Billy Malone slid off his saddle. Slocum caught him before he fell. "I can't go on. Too tired, too weak. Best you go without me," Billy said.

"No, put him up behind me and tie his legs to the saddle. He can hold me," Theresa said.

169

Yanuza held his ear to the ground. "Many horses," he said.

"Follow me," Das-Te-Sah, said. She led the way down the bank and into the irrigation ditch. Yanuza swept earth over the hoofprints, then led his horse along the other side of the ditch to leave a false trail.

"We must head north," Slocum said.

"First, we must go to the mountains and hide," said the Indian woman. She led the way, trotting and then walking to rest the horses. They traveled across a barren desert and a rock shelf to a small canyon that led to a plateau and deeper into a range of rough mountains.

As Billy rested his head on Theresa's shoulder and folded his hands across her waist, the tops of his hands brushed her breasts. Her horse had an easy gait, and Billy was at ease for the first time in many months. "I hope you don't mind," he said.

"It feels good to be with a man," she said.

"You risked your life to set us free."

"I had no life. My father treated me like a slave. I have not met good men, like you and the doctor," she said.

Billy brushed his lips against her neck and ear. "If we live, I will take care of you," Billy said.

In the morning they came to a range of snaggle-toothed peaks that rose abruptly from the plateau. "The Spanish call these the Sierra Emedio Mountains. My people once lived here. The Spanish are afraid of this place," Das-Te-Sah said.

The horses nickered at the smell of water, and soon they splashed across a small stream and into a thicket of cottonwood trees. "Rest the horses. I must look about," said the Indian woman.

Billy rested his head on Theresa's shoulder. His eyes were closed, and his grip about her waist loosened. She turned and caressed his face. "Be strong. We are almost to safety," she said.

Yanuza ran back on their trail and did not return until the sun was high and shafts of light penetrated into the depths of the canyon. "Many men on horses," he said.

Das-Te-Sah led them into a brushy side canyon and then through a scattering of boulders to a narrow slit, partly hidden by tall grasses, that grew along a stream. "Through here," she said. They emerged into a wider canyon surrounded by high cliffs. The mouths of man-made caves behind rock walls lined ledges a hundred feet above the canyon floor. "The ancient ones lived in this place," the Indian woman said.

Yanuza slipped away, taking his bow and arrows. He made no sound and left no tracks. He returned at dusk with a young deer slung over his shoulder. Das-Te-Sah made a small fire and boiled corn with bits of liver and heart. "This will strengthen your friend," she said.

Theresa fed Billy the stew. Later in the night, when he had a shaking chill, she wrapped him in her saddle blanket and warmed him with her body. The next morning he burned with fever and his skin had a yellowish tinge. Das-Te-Sah made tea from the bark of a willow, but it had no effect on the fever. Tom Slocum ran his hand over Billy's belly and found an enlarged spleen. "Billy has malaria, the worst kind. He will die without quinine. We need to find a village," he said.

"The Mexicans will catch us if we go to the valleys. We must stay in the mountains and go north," the Indian woman said.

"No, please, no, we must find help," Theresa said.

"The priest in Opunto may help us if he has quinine. Otherwise, Billy will die," Tom said.

"We Apaches leave our sick ones behind. Perhaps you have a better way," Das-Te-Sah said.

While there was still light, Das-Te-Sah found a narrow trail that led out of the canyon. Tom and Yanuza had lifted Billy onto Theresa's horse and tied his hands around her waist. His head lolled against her shoulder and jerked each time the horse stumbled or jumped to a new foothold. The Indian woman led them higher on the steep wall of the canyon, and it was full dark when they came out on top of a low mesa and made a fireless camp. Billy shivered with chills, then burned with fever, Theresa wrapped him in her blanket and protected him from the cold. They waited until late afternoon before crossing the desert between two great sand dunes. "The village with the priest is there," Das-Te-Sah said, pointing to the northeast. "You go, the boy and I will follow and keep watch."

When they approached the village, dogs barked, but the ruckus did not arouse sleeping peons. Tom led the way to the stable behind the church. He and Theresa half dragged and half carried Billy to the door of the old priest's adobe house. Slocum knocked gently until a voice said, "*Un momento.*" Father Alonzo opened the door and held a lighted candle.

"Who are you?" he asked.

"Dr. Slocum. We need help."

"Your voice, you are the doctor who gave me sight. Now I can see your face. Come in."

"My friend is very sick. He must have the bark of quinine."

"I am so happy. You performed a miracle. I can see again. Come in. How can I help?" Father Alonzo asked.

"I found my friend, but he is dying with malaria. He must have quinine," Slocum said.

"You are in great danger. Don Diego's men have been in the village. He will pay one thousand pesos for each of you. The people would do anything for the money."

"We must save my friend. Do you have quinine?" Slocum asked.

"I believe so. It is also called the Jesuit's bark. Ah, yes, in this jar."

"Please, we must hurry," Slocum said.

They put Billy on the priest's cot, and Theresa covered him with blankets. Father Alonzo crushed the dried, brown Peruvian bark in a mortar, added coarse brown sugar, ground it into a powder, and added boiling water. When it was ready, he poured the mixture into a cup and added blood-red wine. "It is very bitter and must be taken in sweet wine," he said. Theresa held Billy's head, while Slocum forced spoons filled with the medicine into Billy's mouth. He made a feeble effort to swallow and took in a third of the cup.

"It is enough. Let him rest," the priest said. Father Alonzo lit the fire and heated beans with bits of pork. Slocum and Theresa ate and then fell asleep on the floor. At daybreak, Billy

172

stirred and took more medicine and a long drink of water. Father Alonzo was troubled when he returned from his morning walk. "Don Diego's men found the tracks of your horses. You must hide."

"It is too soon to move my friend," Slocum said.

"They will search the church. Come with me. Take food, the medicine, and candles," the priest said.

Billy's skin was cool, his pulse slower, and he was able to get out of bed. Theresa helped him follow Slocum and Father Alonzo into the church. The priest pushed aside the statue of the Angel of Guadalupe and lifted an iron ring set in the floor. Stone steps led down into a black cave. "Down there," he said.

The narrow crypt was lined with deep niches dug into the walls that contained rotted, ancient coffins. Skulls with bits of clinging hair and bones lay in the dirt. Father Alonzo closed the stone and slid the Virgin of Guadalupe back in its place. The crypt widened to a small room smelling of decay. Theresa gave Billy another dose of quinine, a morsel of bread, and hugged him close. Hours passed while they dozed or stretched aching limbs.

Sandaled feet scuffled overhead, boots thudded on the church floor, and a muffled, angry voice shouted, "Priest, my men saw the gringo bastards in this village. You can have money for a new church," Don Diego said.

The candle had long since guttered out when the stone ring slid open. "It is safe to come out," Father Alonzo said. They crept through absolute blackness to the stone steps and up into the dim church.

"Don Diego would have killed me and the people, but even he respects the Angel of Guadalupe. He left us alone. It is another miracle," the priest said.

"Has he left?" Slocum asked.

"I led your horses to the edge of town and let them loose. Don Diego and his men went away to the north, but he may have left spies in our village," Father Alonzo said.

Theresa genuflected. "Thank you, Father," she said.

"You can rest today but must leave tomorrow night," the priest said.

CHAPTER NINETEEN
The Last Stand

While Slocum held the reins, a village boy helped Billy onto Father Alonzo's mule. The old priest led them through an alley to a small orchard beyond the cluster of adobe huts. "Make haste. Keep the North Star on your right hand. You will cross a bean field to a ditch at the edge of the desert. Beyond are the mountains and safety." Father Alonzo made the sign of the cross. "God bless your journey and take care of the mule; she has been a faithful servant of the Lord."

The village dogs lifted their heads, sniffed the air, and raised the alarm with raucous barks and howls. The noise, as well as his bursting bladder, aroused one of Don Diego's men from a drunken sleep on the floor of the cantina. He stumbled out the door, and as he shook away the last drops of urine, he caught sight of the priest giving his blessing. It had to be the Americanos and the woman. He could almost feel the reward money jingling in his pocket.

Slocum led the mule with Billy at a trot, but after they crossed the bean field, Theresa lagged, and Slocum paused to let her rest. A coyote yipped. Slocum answered with the shriek of a dying rabbit. Yanuza rose from his belly twenty feet away and held his hand, palm out. Das-Te-Sah led her mule and a horse from the shadows of willow trees along an irrigation ditch. "One of Don Diego's men may have seen you," she said.

Theresa and Billy mounted the horse, while Slocum and the Indian woman rode the mules. Yanuza cast aside his Mexican clothing for the leggings and breechclout of a warrior. His bow and the old Sharps rifle were strapped to his back, and he carried the Mexican repeater at the ready. They set off across the desert at a good pace. The Indian boy ran with an effort-less stride and easily kept ahead of the riders until he dropped behind and climbed a sand dune to look out for followers. When they reached shelter of a small canyon in the foothills, Yanuza came at a flat-out run but breathed easily and spoke rapidly with Das-Te-Sah.

"The boy says there are many men on fast horses." Das-Te-Sah pointed up a boulder-strewn slope that ended at a cliff, with the craggy mountain looming higher against the clouds. "We go there."

Das-Te-Sah rapidly removed the paniers from the mules. "We leave everything and go fast," she said.

They put Billy on the Indian woman's sure-footed mule. Theresa mounted the priest's ancient, gray-whiskered mule and started up the slope. Das-Te-Sah took the reins of Billy's mule and led the way. Slocum led the horse, but the frightened animal snorted, slipped on a loose rock, and went down on his haunches when his footing gave way. He struck a boulder the size of a man's head that tumbled away until horse and boulder skidded downhill in a full-scale rockslide. Slocum jumped from rock to rock to keep up with the Indian woman and the mules. Theresa's mount side-slipped; she fell, got up, and fell again. "I can't go much farther," she said. Das-Te-Sah pointed to a ledge with a depression against the rock face of the mountain.

"Go there and stay out of sight. Give me the fast-shooting rifle," she said. Slocum led the two mules from rock to rock up the slope and pulled the mules with Theresa and Billy to the wide ledge against the face of a cliff.

Slocum shaded his eyes from the rising sun and counted at least twenty men spread out at the base of the hill. Don Diego dismounted and studied the slope with field glasses. At his command, the men swarmed up the hill, dodging from boulder to boulder. The Indian woman and Yanuza crawled to positions well below the ledge. When the Mexicans were less than fifty yards away, they opened fire. Yanuza knocked down a running Mexican with the first bullet from the old Sharps. Das-Te-Sah hit another before the Mexicans took cover.

After a lull, Don Diego shouted, "*Valientes, un Americano, dos mille pesos* [Two thousand pesos for one American]!" The Don's men set up a great shout and rushed the hill. Yanuza fired until there were no more cartridges for the Sharps, then, with the Mexican repeater, killed another of the Don's men. The gun jammed. Yanuza screamed the Apache war cry, stood in plain sight, and sent a half dozen arrows into the Mexicans.

Das-Te-Sah rose from her hiding place, stood between two boulders, and emptied the Winchester at the Don Diego's men. She raised the rifle with both hands and screamed, "*Hijos de putas* [Sons of whores]!" She crumpled backward, struck by a Mexican bullet. Slocum left the ledge and crawled on hands and knees, then at a dead run, to the Indian woman. Blood gushed from a wound on the left side of her abdomen.

Oh God, it is either the spleen or kidney, he thought. He ripped a piece from her dress and jammed it into the wound. Yanuza came to her side and cradled the dying woman in his arms. Her dark face softened when she turned to the young Indian.

"You must trust the doctor, walk the white man's way. We are finished," she whispered.

Slocum touched her face and ran a finger over the slightly raised scar on her nose. "I promise to care for him," he said. Das-Te-Sah took one last shallow breath, and then there was nothing.

Yanuza danced on top of a boulder, his arms and legs pumping up and down, with his body stooped almost to the ground. He sang the Apache death chant. Bullets splattered against the rocks, but the Mexicans were shooting uphill and aimed too low. Or was the boy enchanted?

Slocum, in a fit of rage, drew the Don's Colt and downed two Mexicans, but driven by the Don's threats and promises, his men charged. Yanuza grabbed the old buffalo gun and jammed it under a rock half the size of a horse. He heaved until the boulder crashed down the slope. He levered another and another until half the mountain thundered down on Don Diego's men. A shower of stones struck those who ran, but Don Diego with a half dozen men scrambled to one side and found shelter.

Slocum and Yanuza raced to the ledge. "Take the Colt and hold them for half an hour. We have a chance. Come!" Slocum shouted. Yanuza took the revolver, a dozen cartridges, and went down on his belly behind a boulder.

"Can't go farther," Billy said.

"Damn you. I came halfway across the country to save your worthless hide. Get on the mule," Slocum said. He led the mules with Billy and Theresa along the ledge that curved around the face of the cliff to a saddle between two peaks. Gray clouds rolled in from the west, lightning stabbed a distant mountain, and fat raindrops poured out of the sky. A faint trail led downward away from the cliff, and instead of loose rocks, there were clumps of grass, brush, and an occasional stunted tree. Slocum went on, leading both mules. He looked back, but Yanuza had stayed on the ledge. Then came the sound of rifle fire and the distinct *boom, boom, boom* from the Colt revolver.

CHAPTER TWENTY
Geronimo Surrenders

They came down to a level plateau between two mountains that overlooked a stream, which, if he remembered correctly, could be the Nacozari River. It was a desert oasis with scattered islands of trees amidst high grass and brush. The rain had settled to a steady downpour, driven by a brisk wind. Billy shivered, and Theresa was glassy-eyed with fatigue. Slocum had a pounding headache, and Yanuza had not appeared. Had he stopped the last of the Mexicans? Slocum caught Billy when he slid off the saddle, and he dragged him to shelter beneath the boughs of a fir tree. When Theresa crawled in after them, Billy took her in his arms and they nestled together.

Slocum slept fitfully through the night and awoke to muttering voices. It was still drizzling rain, but there was enough light to see Yanuza with three Indian women huddled under blankets. Slocum rubbed his eyes and pointed at the women. "Who are they?" he asked.

"From Geronimo's band. The women are tired and hungry and are searching for the American officer. They say Geronimo wants to surrender," Yanuza said, in a combination of Spanish, English, and sign language.

The quinine had driven away Billy's fever, and a night's sleep, even in the mud and rain, had helped, but Theresa was bedraggled as a bird with a broken wing. She shrunk back from the Apaches, but Billy held her close. He spoke in the Apache language with the women. They had no food but gave a blanket to Theresa. "The women say Geronimo is tired of running and is afraid the Mexicans will massacre his people. He is ready to talk peace," Billy said.

Yanuza found the mules, and the Indian women led the way to the northeast. At noon, they rested by a small stream that tumbled between craggy mountains toward the Bavispe River.

The eleven warriors with cocked rifles appeared by magic from a clump of bamboo cane. Billy raised his right hand, palm forward, and spoke in Apache. "We are friends, have no guns, and mean no harm. The women say you will speak with the Americans."

The Indian camp was hidden in a canyon with good water and grass for the animals. There were many women and children and a few old men in the bedraggled band. They had little food, but the women shared roasted venison and a bread made with acorns. The women who spoke Spanish chattered with Theresa.

The camp went silent when Geronimo stepped out at the edge of camp. Despite his age, Geronimo was as well-muscled as a young buck. His thin lips were set in a hard line across his creased, dark face, and his eyes were black as nuggets of coal; his hair, in two braids, hung down to his shoulders. He cradled a fine Winchester repeating rifle in his arms, and a Colt revolver was thrust into his belt. The old medicine man radiated an aura of power. Geronimo had for thirty years fought the Mexican and American armies. He had never been struck by a bullet and had never been defeated in battle. He walked to Billy Malone, thumped his chest, and spoke in good English.

"I know this man. He is good to my people and was brave in battle with the Mexicans. He did not surrender. The Mexicans took him by treachery when they killed my friend Crawford."

Geronimo's eyes lit on Yanuza. "You have grown strong. Have you been in battle?" he asked. Yanuza thrust out his chest and told of rescuing Billy and the battle with Don Diego's men.

Geronimo clapped both hands on Yanuza's shoulders. His black eyes pierced the very soul of Yanuza. "My son, you are a true warrior, but we fight no more. Our days have ended. We shall surrender to *Bay-chen-dayson* [Long Nose, the Apaches' name for Lieutenant Gatewood]."

Geronimo swept his hand to the mountains and the stream. He spoke in Apache, which Billy later interpreted. "You, the last warrior, must remember *nohwiza'ye bike'e* [our ancestors' tracks]. Our wisdom is in places, and each place has a name, and the name tells a story of our people. See that mountain over there, don't forget the name, *Dzil Ndeeze* [Long Mountain], because it marks this spot where the grandmothers planted corn by good water. Remember this. Warn our people of the bad places so they stay out of trouble. One time, the women and children drank from a stream. The water looked good, but the people became sick. An old man found the place where coyote pissed in the water and made it bad. That place is named, *Ma'Tehilizh*e, [Coyote pisses in the water]." Geronimo went on, imparting tribal wisdom to Yanuza, perhaps the last Apache warrior.

Geronimo and his men broke camp before dawn. The rest of the men, the Indian women, and children left midmorning. Theresa and Billy rode mules side by side, their legs touching.

The Americans were camped at a bend in the Bavispe River near the Teres Mountains. Lieutenant Gatewood and his two interpreters were having breakfast. Tom Horn and some twenty scouts were mounting up to go on patrol. Gatewood flung aside his coffee dregs.

"Is that you, Bill Malone? You're supposed to be dead," he said.

Billy was skin and bones, with a long beard and unkempt hair, and his skin had a greenish pallor. "It's me alright, thanks to Tom Slocum. Can we have some of that bacon and beans? We are about done in," Billy said.

The cook rustled up grub. It felt fine to fill up on bacon, hardtack, and beans, and about a gallon of coffee. "I am about to bust with all this food," Slocum said.

Theresa shrieked like she was getting scalped. There had been no sound, not even a leaf rustled, when the twenty or so Apache men with cocked rifles came out of the brush and surrounded the camp. Yanuza was in the group with a new rifle. They could have killed every American.

Gatewood, as cool as could be, dropped his gun belt and raised his hands, palms forward, and spoke Apache. "We shared our food with your women and have plenty of tobacco for you," he said. Tom Horn and Martine, an Apache interpreter, passed out tobacco and paper for cigarettes. The Apaches rolled smokes but kept their rifles.

Geronimo then came out of the brush, put his Winchester down, and walked to Lieutenant Gatewood. "*Anzhoo?* [How are you?]" he asked. They shook hands and sat down.

"The Mexicans will give us food and mescal if we surrender to them," Geronimo said. He looked away toward the mountains, and his hands trembled. "We need time to rest and decide what is best for my people."

"General Miles wants you to surrender. You can join your family in Florida," Gatewood said.

"The Mexicans got us drunk on mescal. We had fun, but they wanted to kill us all. We don't want to go to Florida. We have our own land in the White Mountains and on Turkey Creek. Let us go there," Geronimo said.

"You must speak with General Miles about the conditions of surrender," Gatewood said.

"You have killed my people, taken our land, the agents cheated us on the reservations. We cannot trust you Americans," said Geronimo.

They stopped to eat and smoke. The Apache warriors shook their rifles and fired bullets in the air. Gatewood and the Americans remained silent. At last, Naiche came into the circle.

"This Gatewood came to us in peace. He speaks the truth. We will be better off with our people, even in Florida," Naiche said.

In the morning, Geronimo, Naiche, and their band came into camp and met with Gatewood and Horn. Billy Malone, in a borrowed uniform, stood with the Americans.

"We will meet with General Miles in Skeleton Canyon and throw ourselves on his mercy. We will keep our weapons, and you must protect us from the Mexican army," Geronimo said.

Billy, Tom, and Theresa jogged along together on borrowed horses, keeping pace with the American soldiers. Billy and Theresa whispered together. *They are like lovers*, Slocum thought. It was an easy ride until a band of Mexican soldiers rode up from the south.

"Give us Geronimo. He is a criminal," the Mexican officer demanded.

"No, he is our prisoner of war. He is going with us to the United States," Gatewood said.

The Mexicans drew their revolvers, and both the Apaches and Americans cocked their weapons. "Damned if it ain't going to be another war," Billy said. Gatewood must have had the same idea because he ordered Tom Horn, the scouts, and Lawton's platoon to get on across the border with the Apaches. The Mexicans didn't have a taste for war with the Americans, faced about, and went back south.

A day later, the troop crossed the border and reached Skeleton Canyon. Geronimo and his band came into the camp the next day.

General Miles demanded unconditional surrender, and after a long palaver, Geronimo and his Apaches gave up their weapons. "I guess this is the end of the Wild West," Billy said.

"What are you going to do with all your back pay?" Slocum asked.

"As soon as you do that operation, Theresa and I are fixin' to get married," Billy said.

"It is better to do that kind of operation in a fine hospital. I know just the place, in New Orleans, and that's on the way home to Sandy Ford," Slocum said.

"What are you going to do?" Billy asked.

"First, I am taking Yanuza to the Indian School in Carlisle, Pennsylvania. Then, I figure on heading back to Sandy Ford to see my son, Dan. I might even go to New Orleans and see a woman I know there," Slocum answered.

ABOUT THE AUTHOR

Dr. John Raffensperger graduated from medical school, served in the Navy, trained in surgery, and became the surgeon-in-chief at a Chicago children's hospital. He has published two hundred articles and five textbooks on pediatric surgery. *The Old Lady on Harrison Street, Cook County Hospital, 1833-1995; Two Scottish Tales of Medical Compassion, With a Brief History of the Edinburgh School of Medicine; Children's Surgery, A Worldwide History;* and *The Education of a Surgeon* are on medical history. His works of fiction include: *Ward 41, Tales of a County Intern*, a collection of short stories; *Red Tide*, a children's story; *The Complete Diaries of Young Arthur Conan Doyle*, which was a Kirkus Indie Book of the Month.

ACKNOWLEDGMENTS

Research for this Tom Slocum adventure story started with Candace Heise, reference librarian at the Sanibel Public Library, who—without fail—found material through the intra-library loan system. With no advanced notice, I wandered into the Reference Center for Southwest Research in the Zimmerman Library of the University of New Mexico. Chris Geherin, within minutes, found and duplicated pertinent articles from the New Mexico Historical Review. The Desert Museum, Rodeo, New Mexico, has a wealth of material on desert flora and fauna as well as a room filled with artifacts and weapons that once belonged to Geronimo. Bob Ashley, director of the museum, kindly reviewed the manuscript. The Amerind Museum and Foundation, Dragoon, Arizona, has excellent exhibits depicting Native American culture as well as material on the Southern Apaches and Geronimo. John Amalong, at the Chiricahua Regional Museum in Wilcox, Arizona, kindly shared his personal reminiscences about the Apache territory and explained the museum's exhibits and artifacts. Kate Fitzpatrick, MA, librarian and archivist at the Arizona Historical Society, Tucson, Arizona, kindly allowed me to review the Gatewood file of photographs related to the Geronimo campaigns of 1885-86. My visit to the site of Fort Bowie and the visitor center provided insight into the original fort and the living conditions of the soldiers stationed there during the Geronimo campaigns of 1885-86.

Review Requested:
We'd like to know if you enjoyed the book. Please consider leaving a review on the platform from which you purchased the book.

Lightning Source UK Ltd.
Milton Keynes UK
UKHW040657241221
396187UK00001B/32